Melissa,

a *splash* of VANILLA

♡

Bethany
Lopez

A Splash of Vanilla
Copyright 2018 Bethany Lopez
Published November 2018
ISBN—9781728750712

Cover Design by:
Makeready Designs

Editing by:
Red Road Editing / Kristina Circelli

Proofreading by:
KMS Freelance Editing

Interior Design & Formatting by:
Christine Borgford, Type A Formatting

also by

BETHANY LOPEZ

Young Adult:
Stories about Melissa—series
Ta Ta for Now!
xoxoxo
Ciao
TTYL
With Love
Adios
Nissa: a contemporary fairy tale

New Adult:
Friends & Lovers Trilogy
Make it Last
I Choose You
Trust in Me
Indelible

Contemporary Romance:
A Time for Love Series
What Happened in Vegas (Prequel)
8 Weeks
21 Days
42 Hours
15 Minutes
10 Years
3 Seconds
7 Months
Novella—*For Eternity*

The Lewis Cousins Series
Too Tempting

a *splash* of VANILLA

a *three sisters catering* novel
BETHANY LOPEZ

To my fellow In The Loop Group Authors, thanks for your advice and support. I'm happy to be a part of a group of such wonderful women.

Prologue

"He's gone, Pris."

I was hiding in the pantry, as usual. It was my favorite place to hide, because not only could I shut myself in and get some time alone away from my sisters, but because there were snacks.

I could hear my mom talking, and since she said *Pris*, I knew she must be talking on the kitchen phone to her sister, Priscilla.

I scooted back farther into the pantry, shoving my small, eight-year-old frame into the corner, just in case she decided to open the door and look inside for something.

"I mean, he *left* . . . His clothes are gone, his office is empty . . . he's *gone*. He left us," my mom said, her voice getting high like it did when she was about to cry.

"He's with *her*, I just know it."

I wondered briefly who she was talking about, and why she sounded like she was about to cry, when she never cried, then went back to reading my favorite Nancy Drew book. I was getting to the good part and just had to know what happened next.

I had my flashlight, a bag of cheddar Goldfish, and a Yoo-hoo, I was good for at least an hour.

A couple chapters later, I heard movement right outside the door and looked up to see the handle slowly turning.

The door swung open and my twin sister, Millie, stood there. Her long brown hair was a tangled mess and her face was streaked with tears.

"What's wrong, Mills?" I asked as she dropped to her knees and crawled toward me.

"Daddy's gone," she said, her breath hitching.

I put my book down and pulled her in for a hug.

Her body was shaking with sobs, so I rubbed my hand over her back, hoping it would help.

"What do you mean, *he's gone*?" I asked, my mind wandering back to my mom's phone call with Aunt Priscilla.

Had she been talking about Daddy? And, if so, what did she mean by *he's with her*?

"Daddy moved out, Dru. Tasha said she saw him get into his car this morning and it was full of boxes and suitcases."

That night, Millie and Mom sat outside, waiting for Dad to come home, and this time my mom held Millie while she cried.

Tasha, our younger sister, refused to come out of her room. She didn't eat dinner, take a bath, or even come out to watch TV.

I wasn't angry like Tasha, or sad like Millie.

I was numb. I'd never been his favorite, that was Millie, or the one who got the best grades, that was Tasha. I'd spent my life feeling like I wasn't good enough for him to pay attention to me, so his leaving didn't really mean much to me.

If it had been our mother, well, that would have been different, but our *father*? I never wanted to see him again.

One

Dru

I looked around the banquet room, which we'd converted into a speakeasy for my twenty-ninth birthday party, and forced a smile.

Yes, it was perfect. Decorated exactly how I wanted, *no*, it actually turned out even more awesome than expected, but that didn't change the fact that it was a party to celebrate *my* birthday, not mine and Millie's.

It was the first year since *birth* that we hadn't agreed on a theme, spent hours finding the perfect cake, and argued over who got to open presents first. This year, Millie had requested that we do separate birthdays, with each of us getting to choose our own festivities.

She'd opted to have a small lunch, with just us sisters, Millie, Tasha, and me, along with her boyfriend, Jackson. While I'd gone the more *Dru*-like route, with this big blowout.

I guess that had been Millie's point, that she wanted something more low-key, and didn't want to rain on my party parade, and although I'd said I understood and agreed, it had still hurt my heart.

Everything was starting to change, and I hated it.

Millie was falling for Jackson and had already brought up the fact that we needed to hire more help at Three Sisters Catering, and stop working ourselves to the bone. If things kept progressing, she'd be moving out of her apartment above our shop and in with Jackson, and that would just leave Tasha and me alone in ours.

It also turned out that Tasha had a love affair with Jericho Smythe, the owner of Prime Beef, the restaurant across from Three Sisters, and had kept it from us for years.

Since our mother had died and we'd started a business together, my sisters had been the glue holding me together. This sudden upheaval of my finally established life was making me twitch, and Millie's suggestion to split up our birthday was the icing on a quickly crumbling cake.

I took a deep breath and let it out slowly, swinging my hips so my black fringy flapper dress swayed around my thighs, and tried to let the sound of Louis Armstrong lift my spirits.

"Care to dance?"

I looked up to see a handsome guy grinning down at me.

He was a friend of a client, easy on the eyes, and hell, it was my birthday, so I grinned back, tossed back my drink, and accepted his offered hand.

After a few more dances, and a lot more drinks, my smiles and laughter were becoming genuine, especially when I saw Jackson, decked out in an Elvis costume, pulling my twin through the room.

Although I was fearful of change, I did like Jackson for my sister. He was sweet, funny, and romantic . . . exactly what Millie deserved.

And, since I knew he was about to surprise her with a trip to Graceland for her birthday, I couldn't help but tear up at the thought of how happy she was going to be. Millie had an Elvis obsession and Graceland was on her bucket list. She was going to be over the moon.

I danced until my feet hurt, and drank until I realized how much I loved *everyone*.

It wasn't until Jackson and Millie were trying to wrangle Tasha and me up the stairs that my fears came back tenfold.

Our mom had been gone for over a year, Millie was going to fall in love with Jackson, get married and have babies, and Tasha was probably going to get back together with that Jericho guy, even though they hadn't spoken to each other in years.

Where did that leave me?

I was sitting outside my door while Jackson and Millie tucked Tasha's drunk self into bed, dozing in and out as I struggled to grasp the thoughts flitting through my foggy brain.

"You hold her up and I'll open the door," I heard Millie say, and then I was being lifted and shuffled across the threshold and into my apartment.

I cleared my throat and looked up at Jackson as an idea hit me.

"That guy who found your wife . . ." I began.

"Mick," Jackson supplied.

"Yeah, him . . . do you think he could find our dad?" I asked, then clamped my mouth shut when Millie came back the room.

Jackson's soon-to-be ex-wife was a dead-beat mom. She'd left Jackson and their daughter, Kayla, and had essentially disappeared. Wanting to find her and get a divorce, Jackson had hired a private investigator.

I let Millie usher me into bed and get some aspirin and Gatorade in me, then feigned sleep so that she'd leave.

Once she was gone, I got back up on shaky legs and went to my desk.

I pulled out a pen and paper and wrote down everything I remembered about our father, the last time I'd seen him, and the bits of information I'd heard my mom and aunt say about him over the years.

Millie, Tasha, and I had agreed years ago that we never wanted to see him again. Heck, it had been years since we'd even mentioned his existence, and I knew they would not be on board with me looking for him now.

So, I decided not to mention it. Not yet anyway. I'd get the info from Jackson and contact this Mick, then, if he was found, I'd tell them.

Our father had left our mom years ago to begin a relationship with the woman he'd cheated on her with. For all I knew, we could have more siblings out there. Sure, our dad was a creep, and I had no interest whatsoever in meeting the adulteress he'd left us for, but maybe we had more family out there that we didn't even know about . . . which would be kinda cool.

And, maybe, *just maybe*, I could find out why he left us without so much as a backwards glance.

I stood up and gave a decisive nod.

I was going to do it.

Mick

"*Y*eah, I can do that. I'll be there after I get some work done. And, Heeler, congrats, man," I said, then disconnected the call.

Jackson Heeler was a client-turned-friend, who'd just gotten back from a trip to Graceland with his woman, Millie. He'd called to tell me that they'd gotten engaged and were throwing an impromptu celebration, friends only, tonight at the bar.

I wasn't the kind of guy who did engagement parties and weddings, but I could get down with having a few drinks and playing pool with friends.

I'd hung out with Jackson and his buddies a couple times since I'd closed the case on finding his worthless ex. They were a good group of guys, and their women were funny and cool, so I usually accepted Heeler's offer to hang out, as long as I didn't have a job to do, or a woman of my own to entertain.

"Who was that, Michael?"

"My buddy, Jackson. He and his lady just got engaged, so I'm meeting up with them later," I told my mother as I crossed the small room she called home.

"Hmmm, must be nice, having a son who's ready to settle down with a good woman and have children."

I shook my head, but couldn't hold back a grin.

"Real subtle, Ma."

My mother shrugged, her too-skinny shoulder protruding from the fabric of her well-worn nightgown.

"What's on the agenda for today?" I asked as I helped her ease into her favorite chair.

"There's a pinochle tournament this afternoon, and tonight they're showing *Moonstruck*, with Cher, in the rec room," she replied, taking the remote I offered and turning on the TV.

She stopped on one of the court room shows she liked and I went to fill her water bottle with sweet tea.

"You gonna go?" I prodded, biting back a curse when I saw she was low on Little Debbie Snack Cakes. I'd forgotten to pick some up on my way over.

"I don't know. Last time I played pinochle, I swear Robert was cheating. Ain't no fun playing with a cheater."

I chuckled as I handed her the drink.

"You know, if you move in with me, I'll teach you how to cheat at cards," I said, trying the same thing I did every time I came to visit, to get her to leave this damn home and stay with me where she belonged.

"You better not be cheating at cards, Michael O'Donnelly, I raised you better than that," she chastised.

I crouched on the floor next to her and took her hand in mine.

"Come on, Ma, let me take care of you. You deserve better than this place."

I ignored the fact that my mom's eyes got misty, cause she'd be pissed if I pointed it out, and squeezed her hand gently.

"This place is fine, son. I have friends, my own space, and as much Jell-O as a person could ever want. You need to be on your own, havin' space to bring a good woman home too, not sharing that place with your mother."

She pulled her hand from mine, then patted the top.

"Any woman worth my time would understand that you deserve a place in my home. After all, I had a place in yours for almost twenty years," I argued, knowing she was going to reject me just like she had ever since deciding to sell the home she'd lived in for sixty years and moving into this assisted living home.

"I love you, Mickie," my mom said, turning her attention back to the TV and effectively ending the conversation until next time.

"I love you, too, Ma," I replied, standing up and going to make her bed.

I straightened up her room, like I did during every visit. Made sure she had a few paperbacks on her nightstand, a drawer full of Jolly Ranchers, and a full pitcher of sweet tea.

"I'll run by the store tomorrow and stock you up. Any requests?" I asked as I grabbed my phone and keys off of the counter.

"My Little Debbie's . . . oh, and I'm running low on body wash."

"Okay."

I bent to kiss her cheek.

"Call if you need anything."

"Have fun at your party tonight."

I nodded at the front desk attendant as I signed out, then walked outside and took a deep breath. I hated the smell of that place. Hated the fact that my mom would rather live there than come home with me. But, my ma had always been a strong and independent woman, and there's no way I'd take the choice away from her and make her move.

Didn't mean it didn't suck every time I left her in that place.

I was about to climb up in to my beat-up old Army Jeep, when my phone rang. I checked the screen, saw it was an unknown number, and pressed accept.

"O'Donnelly," I said in greeting, figuring it was gonna be business.

"Hi, uh, Mick, I mean . . . *Michael* O'Donnelly? My name is Dru, I got your number from Jackson. Jackson Heeler," the woman on the other side said.

Her voice was low, sultry, *sexy*, but I pushed that knowledge aside and kept my tone all-business.

"That's me, what can I help you with?" I asked as I settled into my seat.

"Oh, well, I'd like to hire you . . . to find my father." I heard her take a deep breath. "But, you see, my sisters, Millie and Tasha . . . Millie's the one engaged to Jackson . . . well, they don't want to find him, so I'd kind of like to keep this between us."

"It'll be confidential, that's no problem," I replied, searching my memory to see if I'd ever met either of Millie's sisters.

I didn't think I had.

"Great, thank you," she breathed, obviously relieved. "What do you need from me to get started?"

"Can you come by my office tomorrow morning?" I asked, wishing I had my calendar in front of me. I wasn't one of those people who believed in keeping everything digital. I liked having a good old-fashioned *paper* calendar on my desk.

I was old school like that.

"I have a nine o'clock meeting with a client, but could squeeze it in during lunch. Does twelve-thirty work for you?"

"Yup, you get the address from Jackson, or do you need it?"

"He gave me one of your cards, so I have it."

"Perfect, see you then, Dru."

"Thank you," she said again.

I nodded, hung up the phone, and headed to the office. As I drove, I wondered if Dru would look as sexy as her voice, then pushed that thought to the back of my mind where it belonged.

Three

Dru

It had been a few months since my birthday party. I'd woken up the next day with a killer hangover and had laughed when I'd seen the notes I'd written about my father.

I'd tried to forget about my silly idea to find him, telling myself that we were all better off without him. But, when Millie had come back from her Graceland trip engaged, and Tasha finally got the courage to talk to her ex Jericho and apologized for the things she'd done in their past, I realized that I still yearned to find him.

Even if it was just to ask him why he'd left, how he could go from being a father to three daughters to totally disappearing from their lives, and maybe to tell him that his name was the last on my mother's lips before she died . . . how much I hated him for that.

I decided I had to do it.

So, I'd gotten Michael O'Donnelly's card from Jackson, sworn him to secrecy, and made the call.

Michael's . . . *Mick's* voice had been deeper than I'd expected. Low and rough, bringing the picture of a cop, fighter, or dock worker to mind. You know, *a man's man*, someone burly and rough, the kind of guy who wore a T-shirt and jeans and would rather die than put product in his hair.

That voice intrigued me, did funny things to my insides, but I'd pushed those thoughts away.

He'd agreed to meet me. Tomorrow at his office. And I was part excited, part terrified, and part *little girl lost* at the mere idea of going through with it.

"Dru, you ready?"

I blew out a calming breath and shot my sister, Tasha, a smile.

"Yes, I've got your back, promise," I assured her.

We were heading to the bar for Millie and Jackson's pre-engagement party. It was just going to be us and their closest friends, with a more formal engagement party for everyone else they know happening next week at Jericho's restaurant, Prime Beef.

Since this was the first time since Tasha and Jericho had cleared the air that they'd be in the same room, I'd promised to stick to her like glue and not let anything awkward, embarrassing, or untoward happen.

Still, I could tell she was nervous.

Tasha wouldn't admit it, but I could tell she was still in love with him. But, since the only times I'd been around him they'd been avoiding each other, I was reserving the right to form my own opinion on the guy and decide whether or not he was good enough for my little sister.

As we walked inside, I spotted our group at a long table. Rob, Ty, and Rebecca were all teachers with Jackson. Rob's wife, Jan was there as well, but there was no sign of Jackson, Millie, or Jericho.

I could see Tasha relax as we grabbed seats at the table.

"The happy couple not here yet?" Tasha asked.

"No, not yet," Ty replied. "They were dropping Kayla off with

Jackson's parents, and should be here soon. Rebecca's putting in an order of appetizers and getting a couple pitchers."

Kayla was Jackson's daughter. She'd been a bit of a turd when Mills and Jackson first started dating, but now she was a sweet potato. I was already working diligently to get *favorite aunt* status.

I felt a presence behind me and turned slowly. The hair on my arms rose and I felt a tingle at the base of my skull. I knew something important was about to happen.

Holy shit.

A man was approaching our table. He was tall and built like a cage fighter, with dark hair and a ruggedly handsome face. And his eyes, *holy Toledo, his eyes,* they were the palest, most striking green eyes I'd ever seen.

"What's up?" he said in greeting, his voice deep and rough, and I knew.

That's him. Mick. The PI I hired to help me find my father.

Suddenly, Tasha kicked me under the table. I snapped my mouth closed and cried, *"Hey, that hurt."*

She bugged her eyes out at me and since my shin still throbbed from her kick, I punched her in the arm.

"Ow!" she muttered with a glare, then leaned in and whispered, "I was trying to help you out before drool started dripping down your chin."

I felt my cheeks flush.

"Shut up, I was not drooling."

"You sure as hell were staring at him like he's a medium-rare steak and you haven't eaten in weeks," Tasha hissed.

I rolled my eyes, my gaze snagging on him again before I turned quickly back to my sister.

"Did you see his eyes?" I asked, because seriously, they were that amazing.

Before I could stop her, Tasha lifted her hand and waved her fingers at him.

Kill me now.

"Hi, I'm Natasha, you can call me Tasha, and this is Dru. We're Millie's sisters."

I felt his eyes on mine and shifted toward him.

"Hi," I managed, but it came out like a squeak.

Mick moved toward us, and I felt myself still as I watched him. *For a big guy, he sure can move.*

"Michael O'Donnelly, you can call me Mick," he said in that voice, his hand outstretched.

I looked down at his hand. His large, capable, *manly* hand. I watched Natasha shake it, then kept staring when he offered it to me.

Tasha kicked me again.

"Ouch . . . stop doing that," I said with a glare, thinking if she kept this up she could deal with Jericho on her own. Then I placed my hand in Mick's and said, "Hi."

I don't know how long we stayed like that . . . my hand enveloped by his, my eyes captured in his pale green gaze. But it was more than a few seconds, and I felt my body grow warm and my hand begin to tingle in his.

Finally, he let my hand go and turned away, effectively breaking off our connection.

I let out a deep breath as I watched his broad back walk toward the bar.

"What was that?" Tasha asked, but I was saved from answering by the arrival of Jericho, Millie, and Jackson.

A few minutes later, Natasha excused herself to go speak with Jericho, *like a grownup*, and I moved to see how Millie was doing.

"So, was Jackson's family excited?" I asked my sister.

She was practically beaming when she replied, "Yes, so excited . . . Who are you staring at?"

I blinked and turned from my perusal of Mick to look innocently at my twin.

"What? No one. Just checking out the bar . . ."

Millie narrowed her eyes at me, looked to the bar where Mick was drinking what looked like whiskey, then back at me. Her expression turned sly.

"Mick? Where you just eyeing Mick like he was a Kate Spade bag on sale?"

"No," I protested. "I just met the guy, why would I be staring at him?"

"Uh, cause he's hot? I mean, have you seen those eyes?" She looked between the two of us again and clapped her hands.

"Stop that," I whispered, slapping her hands.

"I like this. You two would actually be perfect together, in a weird way."

This time I narrowed my eyes at her.

"It's settled, I'm gonna hook you two up," Millie said, and before I could tell her *no way*, she walked away.

Crap.

Mick

My daily routine was pretty simple.

Get up at four thirty in the morning, be at the gym by five. Work out, spar, then shower. Grab some breakfast or a protein shake, then head to the office to do some paperwork. Check the email and phone for messages/new clients, do any case-work I can do, and pick up anything I need for Ma.

After my stop in at the assisted living joint, I usually work cases, and if I'm not taken out of town by business, I either meet the guys at the bar for dinner and drinks, pick up a poker game, meet one of my casual lady friends, or just chill at home.

I was a pretty simple and predictable guy.

My routine didn't change much, even if I was out of town on a case.

So, after finishing my workout and showering, I was driving into the office, my protein shake almost finished.

I shook my head as I thought of Jackson and Millie's engage-ment party the night before. It had been low-key, with the lot of us having drinks and food as we shot the shit and occasionally broke off to play pool.

That wasn't the issue, low-key was definitely my thing, the problem came when Jackson's pretty fiancée, Millie, pulled me aside as I was about to leave.

"Mick . . ." I stopped by the door and turned to see her walking toward me with a tentative smile.

I searched my memory, sure I'd already told her congratulations, but worried I'd somehow forgot, and waited for her to get to me.

"Hey, Millie . . . Uh, congrats again on the engagement. Heeler's one of the good ones," I said, just in case.

She looked at me strangely for a minute, and I knew I *had* already congratulated her, but like the class act she was, Millie just put on a sweet smile and said, "Thanks, Mick. He really is."

"You need something?" I asked, not trying to be rude, but it was getting late and four thirty came pretty early.

"Not exactly, I was just thinking . . . We'd love to have you over for dinner one night, maybe invite my sister Dru along . . ."

Subtle she was not.

I glanced over to where Dru was laughing with Ty and Rob.

There was no denying her sister was hot. Hotter than I'd initially thought when I'd heard her voice. All dark hair and sultry eyes, with tanned skin, a fantastic body, and an even better laugh. Dru would definitely fall into the category of someone I'd get to know better.

But *one*, I didn't do blind dates. And *two*, I didn't mess with clients.

Unfortunately, Dru had asked me not to say anything about finding her father to Millie or Natasha, so I couldn't tell Millie my no client rule. And, she was a nice woman, and I didn't feel comfortable telling her I was more into fucking women than dating them.

"Yeah, uh, Millie, dinner'd be great . . . You won't see me turning down a home-cooked meal, but I don't think I'm the kind of guy you want setting up with your sister. Dinner as friends, sure, but that's about all I got," I said, hoping I didn't come off as too much of an ass.

Millie's smile dimmed a bit, but she nodded swiftly and said, "Great. I'll let you know when."

And as I watched her walk away with a spring in her step and smile over her shoulder, I knew she wasn't going to give up that easily.

Millie was still planning to hook me up with her sister, whether I agreed to it or not.

The sound of a car honking behind me pulled me out of my head and back to the present. I waved in apology to the driver, then continued on the way to my office. I parked my Jeep in my spot and unlocked the door, turning on the lights as I walked through the space I'd worked hard to call my own.

I was proud of what I'd accomplished, and loved the fact that my office looked more like a man cave than a place of business. Sure, there was a room in the back with my desk and files, which looked legit, but the common area had plush seating, a big-screen TV, and shelves lining the walls.

I walked over to those shelves, carefully chose a record, and placed it on the player.

Once the room was filled with the sounds of Bob Seger, I grabbed a water out of the fridge in the corner and made my way to my desk.

An hour later, I heard the front door open and looked up to see Dru walk in.

She was all decked out in a pencil skirt and white blouse, her heels tapping on the floor as she looked around my space.

"Come on back," I called, ignoring the way my pulse jumped at the sight of her.

When Dru walked into the back office, I said, "Take a seat," indicating the chair across from my desk.

She did so with a welcoming smile on her face, crossing her legs as she settled down into the chair.

"*Turn the Page*," Dru said softly, and it took me a minute to realize she was talking about the song that was playing.

Shit, she looked like that and knew classic rock? For the first time ever, my no-client rule was looking like a pain in my ass.

"Yeah," I agreed, too caught up in her to say more.

"And, on vinyl, too, huh?"

I bit back a groan and nodded.

"My dad had an extensive record collection and every Saturday morning, he'd wake us up by playing his music loudly. I hated it as a kid, cause I wanted to sleep, but I learned to appreciate the kind of music he listened to, and the sound of a record playing over a digital recording, as I got older."

The woman was God-damned perfect.

Dru looked at me in surprise, and I realized I'd been scowling at her, so I fixed my face and said, "Cool. Your dad at least sounds like he had good taste in music, even if he was a dead-beat in every other area. Tell me everything you can about him."

I picked up my pen and began jotting notes in my notebook as she told me what she remembered about him and the circumstances of his leaving.

"The last time I saw him, Millie and I were eight. He cheated on our mom and when the other woman gave him an ultimatum, he chose her and left us. There was no warning, no clue that there was anything wrong, he was there one minute, and vanished the next. My mom and Millie had a really hard time, while Tasha and I did our best to be strong for them and act like nothing was wrong."

"Do you know her name?" I asked, noting the way Dru wrung her hands in her lap while she spoke. She may say his leaving meant nothing, but she was obviously more distressed over it than she let on.

"Yeah, uh, Susan . . . Susan Riley. He met her on a business trip to Chicago. I always assumed that's where he went."

"And your mother never heard from him again?"

Dru shook her said. Her eyes started to well, but it was like she pushed back the tears through sheer will.

"What else? What was his job? His last known employer? Stats like height, weight, eye and hair color?"

Dru answered my questions dispassionately. I could tell she was closing herself off from the emotion talking about her father had unintentionally brought out.

When I walked her out, I was left with the impression that not only was she a sexy, intelligent, motivated business woman, she was also strong, a little sad, and had fantastic freakin' legs.

Five

Dru

*T*he meeting with Mick had drained me more emotionally than I'd thought it would.

I'd walked in with the intention of showing the buff, sexy Irishman with the unusual eyes just how confident, articulate, and intriguing I was. After our initial meeting at the bar the night before, I was afraid I hadn't made a very good impression and wanted to make up for it.

After talking with Jackson, I knew Mick was single, and although I didn't know him well, everyone else had great things to say about him. He was funny, loyal, and protective, which made sense, considering his job.

I was interested in getting to know him better.

So, I'd gone in ready to put out feelers, to see if maybe he'd be interested in learning more about me as well, then I'd gone and gotten all freaked out about his questions about my dad.

What had I been thinking? I was hiring him to find our father, of course he was going to want to know more about him, about our past. I just hadn't expected to *feel* so much when I answered those questions.

I'd left without making any sort of move at all. In fact, I'd been the opposite of sexy and alluring, I'd been emotionally stunted and morose.

Decidedly unsexy.

I shook it off as I entered Three Sisters. Neither Mick nor I were going anywhere, so I knew I'd get another chance to show him the real me.

Until then, I had a full load of work to focus on, of which I was already behind, due to my appointment at Mick's.

"Hey, how was lunch?" Natasha asked as I walked into the office.

I felt a twinge of guilt.

I'd lied about going to lunch, since I didn't want my sisters to know I was meeting with Mick. Now the drive-thru burger I'd scarfed down on the drive back was sitting in my stomach like a lead weight.

"All right," I mumbled, sitting down at my cluttered desk and turning on the computer. "I probably should have just grabbed something here."

Tasha chuckled and said, "Millie would have killed you if you'd tried. She's in a bit of a tizzy in the kitchen right now."

"Really? Is everything okay?" I asked, putting my hands on my desk to get back up if need be.

"Yeah, she's good now. They had a little trouble with a late de-livery, and Mills was panicking about the event tonight, but Claire came in early and they're back on track now."

"Okay, good," I said, settling back down in my chair.

We had a promotion event that evening at a local insurance agency to celebrate their new president. This was a big event for our company because it was allowing us to branch out in a way we hadn't yet.

Being the go-to catering company for corporate events could only mean big things for us, and we were all a little anxious about it. We wanted everything to go off without a hitch, so I could only imagine Millie's stress level when her delivery had been late.

I'd caught up on all of my emails, had ensured the van was loaded up and ready to go to the event, and was about to check on Millie, when Tanisha, our brand-new manager, and my new neighbor, popped her head in the office.

"Hey, Dru, I was hoping I could ride over with you, get the chance to see the event from set up to tear down, is that okay?"

"Of course," I replied, putting the last of my things in my leather messenger bag. "I'm just going to stop in and make sure Millie's good, let her know we'll see her over there. Meet you outside?"

"Perfect," Tanisha said with a smile.

She'd only been with us a few days, and I'd been the toughest sell when it came to hiring management and assistant management positions, but I could already see that Tanisha was going to be an asset to our company.

"You need me tonight?" my sister asked as I started out. "I was going to get a head start on the Germaines reception."

I thought about it for a minute, then shook my head.

"No, I think between Tanisha and I, we'll be good. Don't forget that the mother of the bride and mother of the groom are mortal enemies, to quote the bride," I reminded her. "So, make sure you divvy up their contributions and work it so they don't have to interact with each other."

Tasha chuckled.

"Yes, I remember."

"Great, see you later, then."

"Kay. Hey, knock when you get home. If I'm still up, maybe we can have a glass of wine or something."

"Will do," I assured her, then walked to the kitchen.

Millie was putting everything into containers and ensuring the hot food stayed hot and the cold food stayed cold. She had her team working diligently around her, and even had a smile on her face when she caught my entrance.

"Hey, Dru, we're just about ready."

"Great, I was stopping in to let you know that Tanisha and I are on our way to the event."

"I'm glad you did, cause there's something I wanted to ask you," Millie said, her eyes shifting slightly.

"What's that?"

"I want to set up dinner at our place next week. You up for it?"

"Sure, why? Is something going on?" I asked, wondering if there was an issue with their formal engagement party that weekend. Maybe Prime Beef fell through . . .

"No, nothing's up, I just thought it would be nice if we had you over for dinner."

"Just me?" I asked, thinking it was unusual for Tasha not to be included.

"Uh, no, we're inviting Mick as well," Millie said, all wide-eyed and innocent.

"Millie," I began, trying to glare at her even though my lips were twitching. "I thought we already talked about this? Mick and I are grown adults, we don't need you to set us up."

"No, I know, Mick already said he didn't want to be set up, it would just be casual . . ."

My breath caught.

"He said that?" I asked, wondering if it was just *me* he didn't want to be set up with, or if he was on hiatus from all women.

"Yeah, but it was no big deal, just said he's not dating right now. Still, I think it would be fun . . . just the four of us."

"I don't know," I replied. If he wasn't interested in me, I wasn't going to throw myself at him. I did have my pride, no matter how hot I thought he was.

"Come on . . . please?"

"Aren't you going to be tired of get-togethers? What with all of the engagement parties?" I asked, trying to change the subject.

"Tired of parties? Who are you talking to? Besides, we can plan engagement and dinner parties in our sleep and you know it. Plus, with all of the stress of the last few months, I could really use a nice relaxing night, and I miss my twin time."

"Oh, sure, you're going to pull the twin card on me? It's not my fault you've been spending all of your free time with Jackson, and now want to live in sin."

Millie batted her eyes and gave me the little pout that had bent me to her will for the last three decades.

"Fine," I said, throwing up my hands, "but only if you make me your short ribs and there's plenty of red wine."

"Done. Thanks, Dru."

I pushed her shoulder playfully and said, "Now, stop distracting me and let me get to work."

Mick

*I*t had been a wild week.

I'd closed a couple cases, made a quick stop in at Jackson and Millie's "official" engagement party, and spent last night with the guys at O'Reilly's, where I'd found out that rather than going on the kick-ass bachelor party trip to Vegas they'd told me about, they were actually surprising Heeler with a co-ed literary bus trip.

Yeah, I told them to count me out of that one.

We'd learned that Jericho and Natasha had finally stopped tap-dancing around each other and were back together, Millie and Jackson were shacking up, and we'd busted Ty's balls about how he should propose to Rebecca.

In other words, it was like a lady's night rather than a stag night, but whatever, I was getting used to it with this crew.

They were much different than the guys I hung out with from the gym, but Heeler and his teacher friends were always good for a laugh, and Jericho had overcome a lot to get where he was today.

I figured it was good for me to be around guys who didn't just drink whiskey and talk shit all night. These were the type of dudes you could be yourself with, no holds barred, and no judgement. They didn't look down at me because I'd rather eat glass than go on a literary trip, and didn't try to give me shit or change my mind either.

They let me be me, and I was happy to do the same.

Now, I was diving headfirst into Dru's case. First stop, her father's office.

"Yeah, I'm looking for Mr. Temple. A Mr. *Johnson* Temple," I said to the pretty young receptionist.

She glanced up, then did a double take and gave me a onceover. When her eyes finally landed on my face, her expression conveying her interest, I gave her a small smile and leaned in toward her.

"Oh, uh, Mr . . ." the receptionist began, running her hands through her long blonde hair.

"O'Donnelly, but you can call me Mick."

I didn't mind laying on the charm while working on a case. Did that make me a dick? Maybe, but it usually got the job done.

"*Mick*," she repeated with a little laugh.

"So . . . Mr. Temple?" I asked again, keeping my voice low, deepening it a bit.

The pretty blonde cleared her throat and made a play of looking around to make sure no one was listening . . . *they weren't* . . . then leaned over the desk to ensure I got an eyeful of cleavage.

"He's out of town . . . on *business*," she whispered, emphasizing business to let me know that wasn't actually the case.

"Do you know where?" I asked, getting an inch closer. Close enough to touch her hand gently.

She looked down at my hand, then batted her big blues at me. "Vegas."

The phone on the desk rang. I half listened as I looked around and picked up her name. *Dani.*

"With Susan?" I asked.

Blondie shook her head then shifted and tilted her chin toward a closed door to her left.

I looked over and read the name plate.

Susan Temple, Marketing Director.

Through the mirror I could see Mrs. Temple standing behind her desk, a phone cradled against her ear as she looked blindly at the wall in front of her.

I turned back to the receptionist and raised an eyebrow.

Really? my eyebrow asked, and she let out a giggle.

"How long is he away on *business*, Dani?"

Dani flushed with pleasure at her name on my lips.

"At least through the weekend. He likes to get his money's worth."

"Do you happen to know where he's staying?"

She bit her lip and tried to look contrite before saying, "There's only one place Mr. Temple stays in Vegas."

I waited.

"The Bellagio."

"Thanks, doll," I said, standing back up and looking once more around the bustling office.

I wondered how a man who seemingly ran a successful business could disappear for almost a week with his side piece, and still stay afloat.

"Hey," Dani called when I would have turned and walked out.

I paused.

"I hope you nail his ass to the wall," she said, her chin jutted out in a show of strength. "I like Ms. Susan. She deserves better."

I nodded, sure that she'd assumed *Susan* had hired me to find out whether or not her husband was cheating, then shot one more glance at Susan's office, before putting on my sunglasses and heading outside.

Looked like I was going to Vegas after all.

Seven

Dru

*T*he bachelor/bachelorette road trip had been a blast, but who knew traveling around on *The Beast*, which is what we'd lovingly termed the luxury van Jericho had rented, could be so darn exhausting.

First, we had to deal with Millie and Jackson being all lovey dovey, which was understandable, since they were the one's getting married, but now that Natasha and Jericho were officially back with each other, they were fused at the hip.

Plus, with those two couples, and Rob and Ty feelin' a definite bromance, I'd been the odd woman out.

Sure, they'd all ragged on me about my driving skills, and always kept me involved in all of the activities, but I'd still often felt very much *alone*.

The only time I hadn't minded my solitary status had been when I was shown my room at the Inn Boonsboro. I stayed in the Titania and Oberon room, and it was the most splendid place I'd ever stayed. I'd especially enjoyed the gorgeous copper tub in my en suite.

Unfortunately, in the midst of enjoying said room, I'd gotten a call from Mick. And no, he wasn't calling to pronounce his attraction to me or ask me out on a date, liked I'd naively hoped when I saw his name on the screen. Instead, he was calling to tell me he had a line on my father, and was on his way to Las Vegas to gather more intel.

I should have been ecstatic by this information. He'd worked fast, faster than I'd imagined when I'd hired him, but rather been being excited about getting what I wanted, I'd totally freaked out.

Even worse, I couldn't talk it out with my sisters, because not only was I not prepared to deal with the backlash, but I didn't want to ruin Millie's big weekend. So, I'd tried to play it off and act like everything was cool, when all I wanted to do was get home, get back to work, and distract myself from what Mick was doing in Las Vegas.

I was currently checking out a new venue space to see if it would be a good fit for an upcoming quinceañera.

We'd been home for a few days, and I still felt like I was playing catchup. Plus, we had Millie's wedding coming up. In other words, my phone had been ringing off the hook for days, and I'd been running my pumps into the ground.

I bit back a sigh when my phone rang again, then felt a little flutter at the sight of Mick's name on the screen.

"Hey, Mick, what's up?"

"Well, I got some photos of your dad in Vegas, and some information on what he's been up to, but, I'd really like to walk you through it all in person."

"Okay . . ."

"The thing is, I had an emergency come up for a client and I'm currently on my way to Philly. Not sure how long I'll be there . . ."

My shoulders sagged in relief at his words.

"Oh, that's no problem, I'm not in a hurry," I said quickly, then hoped I didn't sound like a complete coward.

"You sure?" he asked, his voice deep and gruff. "I could send you what I got if you really want it, but, like I said, I'd like to go over it with you."

"Yeah, I'm sure . . . totally. I can wait until you get back," I replied, thinking how much I'd like to see him again.

"Perfect, I'll hit you up when I'm back in town."

"Sounds good. And, Mick, *stay safe.*"

I wasn't sure why I said that last bit, or how he'd react to me looking out for him, but all he said was, "Will do, doll," and disconnected the call.

I was still smiling when the phone rang in my hand again. It was Tanisha.

"Everything okay?" I asked when I'd answered.

She'd handled things perfectly while we were gone, but I still worried that something she couldn't handle would come up.

"Yeah, I just need you to meet us at Natasha's apartment . . . Can you come soon? It's a family meeting."

"Uh, sure," I said, wondering why *Tanisha* was calling a *family* meeting.

I finished up at the venue with my heart pounding and my palms starting to sweat.

Did Millie and Tasha find out about me hiring Mick? Are they angry with me for locating our dad? Is this some sort of intervention, or do they just want to yell at me?

By the time I reached Three Sisters and bounded up the stairs to our apartments, I'd practically made myself sick with worry. I opened the door to Tasha's without knocking and rushed in, expecting to see them sitting in a circle waiting for me.

But, they weren't.

Millie and Tanisha were standing outside Tasha's bathroom door. They turned toward me as I entered, and the look on Millie's face had my heart plummeting.

"What is it? What's wrong?" I asked, rushing toward her, my mind automatically going to worst-case scenarios.

"She's in there taking a pregnancy test," Millie whispered, her eyes wide with shock.

"Five actually," Tanisha added.

"She's in there taking *five* pregnancy tests," Milled amended.

"*What?*" I whisper shouted back.

Suddenly, there was a pounding on the door and it flew open to reveal Jericho looking half-crazed.

"Where is she?" he demanded, and the bathroom door flew open.

Before we could say anything to our sister, she flew out of the bathroom and into Jericho's arms, crying and talking all at once.

Jericho was stunned, but remained strong and steady, and I felt tears well in my eyes at the expression on his face when he asked, "You're pregnant?"

"According to this and the four others, yes, but I need to make an appointment with a doctor to be a hundred percent sure."

Jericho turned all business at that, and we stood there watching and he told Tasha everything that was going to happen next. They were going to make an appointment, he was going to move her out of the apartment and into his house, and they were going to get married.

If I wasn't so shell-shocked, I would have laughed at Natasha's expression, but mostly, I was so happy that she was getting the family she'd always wanted, with the man she'd always loved.

She was giving him shit about his lack of proposal, when Millie and I could no longer hold back. We started clapping, shouting, and laughing, all while jumping up and down with excitement.

"We're going to be aunties!" I shouted as I hopped my way over to her and threw my arms around her and Millie.

Knowing it was time to forget the past they shared and finally accept that Jericho was going to be in my family, and that wasn't going to change anytime soon, I let go of my sisters and gave him a quick hug of congratulations.

I could still feel his stunned gaze on me as I ushered Natasha downstairs to get some food and make her appointment with the OB/GYN.

"I can't believe you're moving in with him," Millie said as we walked down the stairs.

"Well, everything he said in his non-proposal made sense. We practically lived with each other in college, and we've wasted so much time already, I don't want to waste anymore. Plus, I think it's sweet that he doesn't want to miss any of the pregnancy."

"Sure, it's sweet, but that means I'm going to be here alone," I cried, trying to make it sound like a mock-whine, even though I really was upset at the realization that both of my sisters were leaving me here alone.

"You're not alone, Tanisha is here," Millie countered.

"Yeah, and, if you want, we could always rent out my place, too, that way you have two new neighbors."

"Yeah, I guess, but I get to choose who moves in," I said.

"Deal," my sisters said in unison.

Eight

Mick

*S*hit was hitting the fan in Philly.

The client that brought me to Philly was actually Jericho. He'd hired me to find his mom, who'd recently got out of jail, because he was worried about her making trouble for him and Tasha.

I'd gotten a lead on a place where Jericho's mom had stayed right after her release, but the guy, Gregory, said he'd kicked her to the curb a couple weeks ago. Couldn't put up with any more of her shit.

Next, I'd gone to see Mrs. Smythe's parole officer, to see when their next meeting was. Once I told him about her call to Jericho, he said he'd schedule a meeting with her for ten the next morning, just to make sure she was where she was supposed to be.

So, I went back to my motel, thinking I'd finally get some shut-eye, then close this shit out for Jericho after I talked to his mom.

Unfortunately, that's not how shit went down.

I'd been having a pretty hot dream involving Dru and a can of whipped cream, inappropriate, sure, but it wasn't like I had control over my dreams, when the phone rang and pulled me out just as things were getting good.

"Smythe," I barked into the phone when I saw it was Jericho.

The man needed to learn a little patience.

"Sorry to wake you, but Natasha is gone. Have you found my mother?"

Before I could respond, the line went silent.

"Smythe!" I yelled into the phone. *"Jericho?"*

I was about to hang up and call him back when I heard him say, "Mick, it sounds like my mom was here . . . I'm guessing she has Natasha."

I explained about my conversation with the parole officer and that his mom would have to be at that meeting, or face the consequences.

"I'm getting in the car now," he said, and I could hear him frantically moving around.

"No," I said loudly, my tone firm. The last thing I needed was a man on the edge coming in and messing things up. "You hired me to do a job, let me do it."

"Fuck!" Jericho yelled, and I knew he was going to listen.

A minute later, Jericho's best friend and sous chef, Hector, took the phone.

I explained why I needed them to stay put and let me handle things on my end, and got Hector's word that he'd keep Jericho in check.

When Jericho took the phone back, I assured him, "I'll bring her home, Jericho, yeah?" Then, for whatever reason . . . maybe because I'd just been dreaming about her, or knew she'd be worried about her sister and wanted to make sure she was okay, I added, "Tell Dru, too."

If he thought that was a strange request, Jericho didn't say so, he just agreed to tell her, and when I told him I'd call as soon as I got news, we hung up.

After that call, I wasn't able to go back to sleep, so I spent the night following dead-end leads. I was in a local diner pouring coffee down my throat and waiting on my eggs, when I answered a call from an unknown number.

"Yeah this is Gregory," he began, and I pushed back from the table. "The girl, Natasha, is here."

"Is Smythe?" I asked, walking to the register as I pulled out my wallet.

"Sir, your food just came up," the waitress said as she ran over to meet me at the register.

Gotta go, I mouthed as I pulled out cash.

"No, she went to see her PO. She won't be gone long, so you'd best hurry."

I dropped the cash on the counter and walked out, eager to get to Gregory's before Jericho's sorry excuse for a mother returned. This may be my only window to get Natasha without things getting messy, and I knew I had to take it.

As I drove, I called the parole officer and told him what had happened. Her leaving town, breaking into her son's house, and abducting Natasha and taking her across state lines. Needless to say, Mrs. Smythe had just gotten herself a one-way ticket back to jail.

Still, I wouldn't feel good about it until I had Natasha safely with me.

I ran up the steps of Gregory's crappy apartment and knocked on his door. When he opened it, I stepped inside and surveyed the space until my gaze landed on Natasha. She looked scared shitless in a robe, nightgown, mismatched pajama pants, and thick socks.

She let out a relieved gasp when she saw me and ran toward me like her ass was on fire.

I caught her in my arms and held her as she struggled to keep it together.

"There's a lass," I said gently, then looked over her head and said, "Thanks, Gregory."

I led her down the stairs, out the door, and got her settled in my work truck.

I shot off a text to Jericho, telling him his girl was safe and that we'd call soon. We waited until the PO confirmed that he had Mrs. Smythe in custody, then took off, not looking back, eager to get the hell out of Philly and back home.

Once we were finally on our way, I handed Natasha my phone and suggested she call Jericho. I knew he was likely waiting by the phone.

I tried not to pay attention to what she was saying, wanting to give them their private moment, but when Tasha started crying uncontrollably, I took the phone from her hand and assured Jericho that although she was shook up, Natasha was unharmed, and we'd be back as soon as possible.

She laid down on the seat next to me and dozed off, sleeping most of the drive.

When we pulled up to Jericho's, everyone was waiting, and Natasha was barely out of the car before he was there, holding her, kissing her, and promising to kill his mother.

I hung back, letting them go inside before following.

I'd just walked in the door and shut it behind me, when Dru was there.

"Thank you," she said softly, then, before I knew what she was about, Dru put her arms around me and pulled me in for a tight hug, much like her sister had.

I knew it was inappropriate of me to cradle her gently against me, it went against all of my rules, after all, but I couldn't quite stop my arms from holding her close and my lips from brushing across the top of her head.

I inhaled her fresh, sweet fragrance, closing my eyes for the briefest moment to commit it to memory, then I pulled back and let her go.

"Just doing my job," I said, but she just shook her head and gave me a small smile.

"It means more than that to us . . . to me. Thanks for being there, and bringing her home safely."

I didn't reply, just watched as she walked away, then went into the kitchen, accepted the beer Jackson offered, and followed him out onto the back deck where there was a fire going in the pit.

A few seconds later, Jericho came out and threw the outfit Natasha had been wearing into the fire, and I handed him a beer.

"Cheers," the three of us said, then we watched in silence as the cotton turned to ash.

Nine

Dru

*T*raumatic events can often make living in the moment seem that much more important.

When you realize how things can change in an instant, that one moment you can be safe and sound in your bed, and the next you can be abducted and driven across the country with an unhinged ex-junkie, you may decide you don't want to wait another second for the *good* in life.

That was the case with Natasha and Jericho.

Once she went to the doctor and was positive that both she and the baby were healthy, Natasha decided not to live another minute not being Jericho's wife.

Although Millie and Jackson had graciously offered to share their special day with Natasha and Jericho, they decided not to wait to have a big wedding, but to go ahead and make an appointment at the Justice of the Peace and get married as soon as possible.

That's why, in the middle of the week on a Wednesday afternoon, Hector and Jackson were standing with Jericho, while Millie and I, along with Kayla, were standing with Natasha, as they vowed to love each other for the rest of their lives.

"I now pronounce you husband and wife."

Natasha was positively beaming in her ivory backless knee-length gown with a lace underlay. Her bright-red bob was recently dyed and cut and styled to perfection. She wore matching strappy heels and a smile that just wouldn't quit.

After the short ceremony, we met the rest of the gang—Mick, Ty, Rob, Jan, Rebecca, and Tanisha—at Prime Beef, for a delicious dinner celebration, which also included the staff of Prime Beef and Three Sisters.

It was a beautiful day, and I was so happy for both Jericho and Natasha.

Although Jericho and I had gotten off to a rocky start, I knew he loved my sister, especially after being with him during the harrowing day of her abduction. I had no doubt that he'd love and cherish her and their baby for the rest of his days.

"You look beautiful."

I turned from the bar, where I was waiting on a champagne refill, to see Mick standing behind me, devastatingly handsome in a perfectly fitted navy-blue suit.

I looked down at my little black dress, which was lacy enough to be a bit dangerous, and gave him a smile.

"Thanks, you look very handsome yourself," I replied, my stomach dipping under his green gaze.

"I can't believe they pulled this together so quickly," Mick said with a half grin. "Good thing I'd already gotten my suit cleaned for Millie and Jackson's wedding next weekend."

I chuckled.

"Yes, we've definitely been going nonstop the last few weeks. Once Millie and Jackson are married, though, we should get some reprieve, at least in our personal lives."

"Yeah, actually, I wanted to talk to you about that . . ."

"Oh?" I asked coyly, hoping and praying that he was going to ask me to be his date for Millie's wedding.

He looked confused for a moment, then ran his hand through his hair and explained, "Yeah, Jackson said you may be able to help me . . . see, my ma's birthday is coming up, and it's a big one, eighty-five. I've been so busy that I haven't had a chance to really think on it, not that I'm the kind to throw a party anyway . . . but, I was hoping I could hire you . . . to throw my ma a party."

"Oh," I said again, the disappointment evident in my tone.

"If you're busy, or you guys don't do those sort of parties . . ."

"No, that's not it," I assured him, trying to smile. It felt tight on my face. "Of course, we can plan your mother's eighty-fifth birthday. We'd be delighted, honestly. After what you did for Natasha, we'll throw you parties for life."

"What was that, then? Your hesitation?" he asked, calling me out rather than letting it slide.

I sighed.

"Honestly? I was kind of hoping you were going to ask me to go with you to the wedding. Not this one, *obviously* . . . Millie's."

Mick winced, which was never a good sign, and nodded.

"*Shit*, Dru . . . it's not that I don't think you're smokin' hot, funny, and just an all-around cool lady, *but* you're my client, and I don't mix business and pleasure. It's kind of a hard and fast rule of mine . . . no dating clients." He ran his hand through his hair again and let out a huff. "I should have made that clear from the beginning, not that I assumed you wanted to get with me or anything. *Jesus*, I'm making a mess of this. It's just, I like you, Dru, *I do*, but I can't be your date to the wedding."

I felt like I was going to throw up. My body flushed with embarrassment, as all hope fled.

"Sure, yeah, I get it," I stammered. "That's probably a smart policy to have."

"We good?" Mick asked. "I don't want shit to get weird between us."

"No, yeah, things are good, of course."

They had to be, considering he was looking for my dad, I'd be planning his mother's birthday, and we shared all the same friends. *Gosh, why did I have to say anything? I should have just kept my big mouth shut, then things wouldn't be so awkward.*

"So, do you have an idea for a theme for your mom's birthday?" I asked, taking a gulp of champagne.

Mick chuckled and replied, "I was thinking a casino night. She and her friends at the assisted living place will get a kick out of it. They always love it when they get to take field trips to the casino."

His mother was in assisted living and he wanted to throw a party there for her and all of her friends? Of course, he did . . . *Because only I would finally find the man of my dreams and have him be completely off limits.*

"We can definitely have a lot of fun with that," I assured him. "Why don't you come by the office this week and we can go over the particulars."

"Sounds great. I've been working your case since getting back from Philly and have some info to share, so I'll shoot you a text tomorrow and we can set up a time and place to discuss both."

As we broke away from each other, I gave him one more glance and wondered where he was in the investigation. Maybe I could find a new PI to find my dad, and then I'd no long be Mick's client, so we'd be free to date . . . or, whatever.

Then I sighed, realizing it was selfish of me to fire Mick from a job he'd already begun, just because I thought we had a connection. I didn't know what his situation was, maybe he needed the money, plus, I trusted him, and couldn't see talking to a stranger about my personal life.

Ten

Mick

"Thanks for meeting me here," Dru said as she took her seat across from me at Rooster's, a little coffee shop down the street from her building.

"No problem," I replied, taking a gulp of black coffee.

"We're pretty swamped today, so I can't break away for too long, so I thought this would be easiest," she explained, and I could tell she was nervous.

Shit, it's probably because she'd admitted she wanted me to ask her out and I shot her down.

"Like I said, it's no problem. I spend most of my time driving around, so it was no skin off my nose to come here."

Dru nodded and took a sip of her frothy steaming drink that was covered in some kind of syrup and whipped cream.

"All right, so here's what I got so far. Your aptly named father, Johnson . . . *cause seriously, this guy's a dick* . . . is living in Chicago with Susan. They've been married about fifteen years and he's had multiple affairs."

"Susan . . . the woman he left Mom for? He's still with her?" she asked, her voice pained.

I nodded and continued.

"Yeah, but like I said, the man can't be faithful. They live together and work together, but he's always on a *trip*. I know they have kids, but I'm not sure yet how many and what genders, although I do know one is a twenty-two-year-old man."

"*What?*" Dru asked, her hand coming out to grab mine on the table.

I could see she was floored. Although she'd mentioned the possibility of having *more family out there*, the reality of it was obviously a bit of a shock.

"Yeah, I can find out the details, or, you can ask him yourself."

"Who?"

"Your father," I said, suppressing a chuckle. She was blinking rapidly, still stuck on the fact she had a brother, and I had to admit, she looked cute as hell.

"Oh, yeah, right. My *father*. So, Chicago, huh?"

"Yup. Look, I know you're busy this week and this weekend is the wedding, but if you wanted to head out on Sunday, do a quick overnighter since you guys are closed on Mondays, then head back, I can make the arrangements."

"You'd go with me?" Dru asked, her eyes finally focusing back on me.

"Of course. I'm not gonna send you off to Chicago on your own." Sure, some clients I might have, but just like with Jackson, Dru was different. Yeah, she was a client, but she was also more. A friend. "I'll make sure he's gonna be home and get us a flight and hotel. All you have to do is pack an overnighter."

She was quiet for a minute and I had a feeling she was having an internal debate about whether or not she even really wanted to meet this asshole, but I could see it in her eyes when she decided that yes, she did, and she could do this.

"Leaving Sunday and coming back Monday will be perfect. The wedding's Saturday night, so we'll be done with that and Millie will be safely on her way to her honeymoon . . . Natasha, too. They won't even need to know I'm gone until they get back and I decide how much I want to tell them."

"Whatever you want," I assured her.

"A brother," she murmured, her tone full of wonder.

"Yeah, at first, I thought Susan was stepping out with a younger man, but then realized it was their son. I did a little digging and learned that he's in college and seems to be a big man on campus type. Plays sports, runs in one of those fraternities, and meets his mother for brunch."

"Wow," Dru breathed, and I could see her eyes start to glisten.

"Do you want me to do more digging, or do you want to ask your father on Sunday?"

She cleared her throat and sat up a little straighter.

"I'll ask him myself. I think we deserve to know that much at least. I mean, I already knew he was horrible for leaving us and never looking back, but to keep our half-brother from us, too, to not give us the opportunity to know him? That's unforgivable."

Her hand on mine started to tremble, so I turned mine palm up and held her hand gently.

"Hey, I'll be right there with you. If it gets to be too much, say the word and I'll get you out of there. This is about you getting what you need, not about him."

"Thank you, Mick, sincerely. It makes me feel better that you'll be there."

She looked like she wanted to say something else, then thought better of it and slid her hand out of mine.

It was probably for the best. I was getting entirely too comfortable touching and holding Dru. I needed that reminder to keep some space between us.

"Now, let's talk about your mother's birthday party."

I grinned, thinking of how surprised my mother was going to be.

"I talked to the admin at my ma's place and they said we could take over the rec room for the evening. Ma loves Poker and Black Jack, so those are a must, but I'm open to suggestion on the rest. Grace, an admin, also said she could make up fake money, and see if they'd be allowed to use it for different things around the complex, but she has to get that approved by management."

"Oh, that would be great, but if that doesn't work we can use casino chips. We have plenty."

"Cool."

"Poker and Black Jack are perfect, easy to set up and execute. We can also rent Craps and Roulette tables, it just depends on the budget. Here's the form we have clients fill out, so that we can determine the theme, which we've already done, as well as color scheme, food, staffing, and, of course, budget. Once I have all of this, I can start planning and making all the necessary arrangements."

"You only turn eight-five once, right?" I asked as I wrote down a number that would buy a car.

I didn't care, I had the money. Saving money had always been a priority for me, and I'd invested well, so dropping a good chunk to give my ma a night she'd never forget was totally worth it to me.

"What about music? Does your mom like Jazz? Or, oh . . . I know . . . a Frank Sinatra impersonator," Dru asked, her eyes lighting up.

"Yeah, she'd love the impersonator," I said, and couldn't help thinking, *she'd love Dru as well.*

Eleven

Dru

Millie and Jackson's wedding was beautiful. Jackson had gotten emotional watching Millie walk down the aisle toward him, and between the look on his face, and the look on Jericho's face as he looked at his new wife, I was beginning to feel like the sad, desperate, doomed to be eternally alone, sister.

Which was why I was ready to turn it up at the reception.

I looked fabulous in my mint-green dress, which Tasha and I had picked out weeks before, and was ready to toss back some drinks and dance until I was the last woman standing.

I didn't begrudge my sisters their happiness, *of course I didn't*, but it still didn't feel good to not even have any prospects, while they were both newly married to the loves of their lives.

I shot a couple longing looks at Mick, who managed to make that suit look incredible, even though I'd just seen him in it at Tasha's wedding. How come men could do that? Buy *one* suit to wear to every event, and get no flack, while if women got caught wearing the same dress repeatedly, it was like there was something wrong with her?

Why couldn't I find the perfect dress . . . one that made me feel sexy, comfortable, and confident, and wear it to everything?

Stupid double standards.

I walked straight to the bar and ordered a Lemon Drop with the sole intention of getting drunk, and made a list of rules for myself.

You will not fawn over Mick.

You will not get so drunk that you throw up.

You will be the funny, fun, party sister, not the green with envy, bitter, crying in the corner sister.

And, again, you will not fawn over Mick. He made his policy clear, and I had too much pride to go after a man who didn't want me.

"Thanks," I told the bartender, then looked out over the prettily done-up space.

We'd gone with an outdoor space and hired a friend I'd met at convention, Laurel. She was from Cherry Springs and owned *Party with Laurel.* When we'd decided to use an outside company, so the staff could come to the wedding as guests, rather than work it, I'd known Laurel would be the perfect choice.

The décor was elegant, feminine, and perfect, just like Millie.

As promised, I drank, danced, gave a touching toast to Millie and Jackson . . . basically had the time of my life, at least, that's what I was projecting . . . and when it came time for the bouquet toss, I was front and center.

I may have elbowed a guest or two, but let out a shout when I caught the bouquet.

Going with the façade of carefree twin, I blew kisses to the crowd and watched with a large grin while Jackson turned and threw the garter right at Mick, who was standing off to the side of the crowd, scowling at his friend.

My stomach dipped when he caught it, and I felt the alcohol

warming my veins as I sashayed onto the dance floor and sat on the chair waiting there.

I looked up at Mick, catching his intense gaze, and saucily put my stiletto on his thigh.

His hand was hot on my bare skin as he pulled the garter up slowly, his eyes never leaving mine.

I could feel my pulse throbbing in my neck, and my breath grew shallow, as my entire being focused on his hand and what it was doing. I didn't care that we had a rather large audience, all I wanted with every fiber of my being was for his hand to keep moving north, while he kissed me for all the world to see.

Of course, that didn't happen.

Once the garter was in place, Mick gave me one last long look, then spun and strode off the dance floor, leaving me sitting there like an idiot.

My face flaming, I stood up, smoothed down my dress and carried my bouquet over to the bar, where I handed it to the bartender and ordered another drink.

"May I have this dance?"

I spun around, half hoping to find Mick asking, even though I knew it wasn't his voice. It was Hector, Jericho's very handsome best friend and sous chef.

"Why, yes, I'd love to," I said, trying for coy, or at the very least, not to slur my words.

I slammed the Lemon Drop and placed my hand in his and let him lead me on to the dance floor.

I'd half expected to do the whole, my hands on his shoulders, his hands at my waist, dance, like in high school, but instead, he took me to the middle of the floor and proceeded to take my breath away as he waltzed me around the floor.

I was no longer pretending to be the fun-loving twin at Millie's wedding, I was grinning broadly at Hector while he spun me around the floor, enjoying the wonderful feeling of dancing with someone who obviously knew what he was doing.

Moments later, Jericho and Tasha joined us.

"Did you guys take dance lessons as kids?" I asked Hector.

"Yeah, it was a good way to stay off the streets, plus, there were lots of girls there," Hector said with a grin, eyes twinkling.

"Ah, makes sense," I replied. I knew a little about Jericho's up-bringing, and that he and Hector had basically grown up on, and survived, the streets of Philly. "I originally started playing soccer as a kid to impress a boy."

"The things we do for love . . ."

I glanced around us, noticing we'd caused quite a disturbance and most of the guests were watching us as we danced, including Millie and Jackson. Jackson's arm was around Millie's shoulder and she was leaning in to him as her gaze moved from me to Tasha and back again.

I smiled at her as I twirled, then I caught sight of Mick standing by the bar. He was holding a glass of amber liquid and frowning in my direction.

"Dru?"

I turned my attention back to Hector and asked, "Sorry, what?"

"I asked if you'd like to have dinner with me some time," he said, and my stomach dropped.

It wasn't that he wasn't extremely handsome, because he was, and it wasn't that he wasn't interesting, smart, and a total catch, but . . .

My eyes landed on Mick again, before shifting back to Hector.

He noticed my hesitation, then looked at Mick and said, "Ah, got it."

I sighed.

"There's nothing happening between us, but . . ."

"You're interested," Hector guessed.

"Yeah, even though he's not."

"I wouldn't be so sure of that."

Rather than argue and give more away than I wanted, I simply said, *"But,* if you're looking for a friend, I'd love to have dinner sometime."

Hector nodded. "I'd like that."

When the dance ended, Hector walked me off the floor, thanked me for the dance, and excused himself.

Deciding the dancing, and probably the booze, had gone to my head a bit, I decided to get out from under the tent and the lights and take a little stroll. If I was going to close down the party, I needed to make sure I didn't fade too quickly.

As I left the sound of the wedding reception behind and faced the trees, I heard movement behind me.

I whirled around to see Mick.

"*Shit*, you scared me," I said with a little laugh, my hand coming to rest over my pounding heart.

Mick didn't stop in front of me like I expected, instead coming right for me and placing one hand on my lower back, while the other tangled in my hair at the back of my neck.

I looked up at him, eyes wide, pulse jumping, and asked softly, "What are you doing?"

"You look so fucking beautiful," he replied intensely, then lowered his head and claimed my mouth.

I gasped, utterly taken aback, and Mick took the opportunity to explore. It was like rockets were shooting off in my body. I was hot, shaky, and eager as I wrapped myself around him like a pretzel and gave as good as I was getting.

I worried that he'd realize what he was doing, remember his rules, and stop the glory that was happening, but he didn't.

His lips were firm, but soft, and he kissed like he was made of testosterone and magic.

It was the best kiss I'd ever had, and if there had ever been any question as to whether or not Mick and I had chemistry, it was squashed. A quivering mess beneath our feet, much like my heart.

Mick's hands never moved, just held me close, the print of his palms searing into my skin like tattoos I hoped would remain forever. My hands, though? They were everywhere. In his hair, on his shoulders, roaming over his biceps, back, and finally . . . his butt.

That's right, I grabbed his butt and squeezed it.

It was the firmest, most perfect ass I'd ever felt in my life, and I found myself wondering what he did to get it that way, when he deepened the kiss and I lost the ability to do anything but live in the moment.

I don't know how long he ravaged my mouth or I violated his body. It felt like seconds . . . hours . . . and I could have stayed there all night.

Unfortunately, like all good things, it came to an end.

Mick

I'd spent the whole day ignoring the elephant in the room, or should I say . . . the elephant in the plane, hotel, and car. I kissed Dru last night, and it was *hot*.

I had no intention of kissing her, had told myself repeatedly since she'd hired me that I couldn't, but seeing her at the wedding, looking gorgeous and dancing like a princess with that guy who works with Jericho, really lit something in me.

Easing the garter up her leg hadn't helped.

I'd almost caved right then, but it was seeing her in the arms of another man that did it.

I was going to leave, had every intention of doing so, then I saw her sneak away from the party and, like a moth to a flame, followed after her.

We'd kissed like we invented the damn act and when I left, it was without saying a word. We'd just kind of *looked* at each other, each backing away slowly, before I turned and left the reception.

This morning, when I'd picked her up to go to the airport to head to Chicago to confront her dad, we'd both acted like nothing had happened.

Except it had. And it had been brilliant. And, we both knew it.

We landed at O'Hare, grabbed our rental car, and stopped by the hotel to check in, then headed right for her father's place.

We'd made chit chat. Talked about the wedding, but had effectively avoided talking about the one thing I was sure was at the forefront of both our minds . . . the kiss.

"Are you nervous?" I asked, still skirting the issue.

"Mmmm, a little," Dru replied, her attention rapt on the city we were passing.

"And what turnout are you hoping for? Just to see him and talk, or is there something more?" I asked, curious, even though it shouldn't matter to me one way or the other.

I never got too personal with clients, but Dru seemed to be the exception to every rule.

She fidgeted with her hands and said, "I don't know if I really have any expectation. I know him enough to know he'd never live up to any of them." Dru sighed. "I guess I mostly want to ask him why he left and never looked back, to tell him that our mom is gone, and to find out about the brother you mentioned. Other than that, I don't want or need anything from him."

I nodded, thinking that was a good answer, but wondering if she was telling the whole truth. Not just to me, but to herself. I worried that there was a piece of her that was hoping her father would take one look at her, pull her into his arms, and promise to be the dad she always wanted.

From what I knew of *this guy*, that was never going to happen, and I didn't want to see Dru hurt.

"All right, well, here we are," I said as I pulled up alongside the curb in front of a large brick house.

I saw Dru take a deep breath as she took in the house.

"Wow, that's big," she said with a raw chuckle. "Quite different from how we grew up."

"Look, Dru, you know it's no mistake that his first name is Johnson, cause the dude's a total dick . . ."

Dru's chuckle warmed me in a way I wasn't prepared to think about, so I kept talking.

"Sounds like you and your sisters were very close to your ma, and wanted for nothing, right? So, maybe your life would have been better if this guy'd been in it, but chances are, he'd have just made things harder, so maybe he did you all a favor by pulling his disappearing act." When she would have protested, I said, "Just gimme a minute," and kept going. "Not to say any of you deserved the shit he pulled, cause you didn't . . . no kid does, but the man can't keep it in his pants for five minutes, and chances are, he woulda just kept hurting your mom, and that wouldn't have been good for any of ya. Look, I'm not saying you shouldn't give him a shot and see what he says, or that you shouldn't miss the fact that your dad wasn't around . . . hell, I miss my pop every day, not that this douche could hold a candle to him . . . but still, I get it. I'm just saying, don't dwell on what you didn't have. Focus on what you did and don't let him get in your head. Get what *you* need out of this meeting. Don't worry about what he's feeling. Okay?"

Dru's eyes were wide on my face.

She reached out and covered the hand I had resting on my thigh with hers.

"Thanks, Mick." She looked back over her shoulder at the house, then back at me. "I think I'm ready."

"I'll be right here if you need anything."

Dru gave me a small smile, then took off her seatbelt and got out of the car.

I watched as she walked up the pretty stone path, which was offset by a perfectly manicured lawn and groomed bushes. There were three steps up to a brick porch with a swing, blue furniture, and a fan hanging from the ceiling. She looked at me quickly, before raising her hand and knocking on the frame of the stain glass door.

I watched as she waited, my own nerves beginning to make my leg bounce.

What the fuck am I nervous about?

The door opened and Susan was there. Tall, blonde, and botoxed, she wore a polite smile as Dru started talking, her hands moving rapidly as she did.

Susan's smile dropped and she took a step back, like Dru was armed or something, yelling over her shoulder as she presumably called for her husband, the man she'd cheated on Dru's mother with.

Instead of Johnson coming to the door, a young, fit, good-looking guy . . . I'm guessing nineteen or twenty . . . slid up next to his mother, a big friendly smile on his face.

This time, Dru took a step back, and since her back was to me, I couldn't tell what her reaction was, but the fact that the boy kept smiling seemed to be a good sign. Susan, however, was not smiling. She spun on her heel and stormed away, leaving Dru, and who I'm guessing was her brother, alone at the door.

He was talking excitedly, and I wanted to roll down the window to see if I could hear what they were saying. After about a one-minute internal battle, I had my finger on the button to do just that, when Johnson finally joined the party.

Except, he was a shitty host.

He ordered his son to leave, and although the boy put up an argument, in the end he shot Dru a grin, said something to her, then turned and walked off, leaving her standing there with their stone-faced father.

When I saw Dru's shoulders droop and the tightness of Johnson's mouth, I murmured, *"Fuck this,"* and got out of the car.

There was no way I was letting her deal with this asshole alone.

Dru

Just breathe, I told myself, Mick's impassioned speech playing in my head on repeat as I raised my hand to knock on the door.

When it opened I was face to face with *her*. My father's other woman. The one who'd taken him away from my mother, *away from us*, and claimed him for her own.

She was tall and blonde, with fake boobs and an obviously touched-up face.

I'd always been terrified of this moment. Of meeting her. Of coming into contact with Susan and finding out she was perfect, or see the glaring reason why we didn't measure up. Except, looking at her now, I realized I'd been afraid for nothing.

She didn't measure up to my mother.

Not even on her best day could she beat my mother's worst.

It wasn't because of her plastic surgery; whatever, it was her body, she could do what she wanted. No, it was in the way she sneered when she realized who I was. It was the utter lack of guilt, or remorse, for what she'd put my family through.

As soon as I explained who I was and why I was there, she bellowed for my father, not bothering to invite me in or even offer a smile. She just stood there, looking at me like I was trash that needed to be taken out.

I was about to open my mouth and unleash every vile thought I'd ever had about the woman, when a handsome young man stepped into the doorway.

His eyes were just like Tasha's.

"Hey," he said, his voice friendly. Then he looked at Susan and asked, "Ma, aren't you going to ask her in?"

Obviously, Susan had raised him to have manners, she just seemed to have forgotten how to use them herself.

"O-kay," he muttered, then shot me a grin and said, "I'm Brody . . . I heard what you said to my mom . . . You're one of my sisters?"

I took a step back, shocked that he knew who I was, barely registering it when Susan let out a huff and spun on her heel to go find my father, who she was still yelling for.

"You know about us?"

"Yeah, just found out recently, actually," Brody said, talking excitedly. "I overheard my parents having an argument . . . When they said something about his other kids I asked him about it. I can tell you, I was completely floored when he admitted to having three daughters. There are three of us, you know . . ."

"*Three* of you?" I asked, my jaw dropping.

"Yeah, me and my two brothers. They're away at school, and I figured it'd be best to tell them in person, you know. I don't wanna drop a bomb like, *we have three sisters*, in a text or something."

Three brothers.

"So, which one are you? One of the twins?" he asked, his

exuberance infectious.

"Yes. I'm Dru. My twin is Millie and our younger sister is Natasha. You're the youngest?"

"Yup. One more year and I'll be free from this place, too. I'm going to school with my brothers."

Before I could ask him more, the breath left my lungs as my father joined us.

He looked exactly the same, yet totally different.

His belly was a little rounder, and there was some gray in the hair at his temples, but other than that, it was him.

"What are you doing here?" he asked coldly, and I felt it like a knife in the gut.

"Dad," Brody chastised, his smile dropping.

"Get inside, Brody."

"I want to stay out . . ."

Before Brody could finish his sentence, our father said, "Now."

Brody glared at our dad, then shot me a grin and said, "I'll be in touch."

I gave him a small smile and nod, then looked at my father.

"Now, I asked *what* are you doing here."

"I . . ." I began, trying to keep reign on my emotions and praying my voice didn't crack, and I could control the tears that I felt burning the back of my throat. "I wanted to find you . . . to let you know about Mom . . . and to . . ."

"I know your mother passed." He paused, and asked, "Is that all?"

A shocked gasp escaped my lips.

How could he be so cold?

"What happened to you?" I whispered, appalled that this man was in any way related to me.

"Look, I don't see any good coming from of you being here.

Why don't you turn around and go back home?"

"Listen up, *dick*."

I turned my head to see Mick storming up the path looking very, *very* pissed.

"Watch yourself, *son*," my father told Mick. "I'll call the cops."

Mick planted himself next to me and stared my father down. He had a few inches on him and looked like he could probably bench press him if he wanted, but my father wasn't cowed. He glared right back at Mick.

"Dru spent time and money to find you. The least you could do is let her have her say. It's not asking much, and she is, after all, *your daughter*. How about you show her a little respect," Mick said, crossing his arms and standing his ground.

I felt his strength and it bolstered my own.

Rather than give my father the upper hand any longer, I looked him in the eyes and said everything I'd wanted to over the years.

"I just want to say that I think what you did was horrible. I think you took the coward's way out, and I don't know how you can live with yourself. I don't know how you thought it was okay to disappear on your family and make a new one, without ever looking back. I wanted to let you know that our mom loved you, to her last dying breath. She was a beautiful person inside and out, and didn't deserve what you did." I felt my eyes fill, but held the tears back. "I wanted to let you know that in spite of you, we're all happy. We had a wonderful childhood and have grown into successful business women. In fact, we run a business together. Millie and Tasha are both married to amazing men who love them, and Tasha is pregnant with your first grandchild, not that you'll ever see him or her. I want you to know that we're happy without you. That we don't need you, and I hope you live a long and miserable life."

I took in a deep breath, shocked by the words that had tumbled out of my mouth, but my dad looked unaffected.

"Is that all?" he asked, and although I wasn't a violent person by any means, I really wanted to hit him.

"I'm going to get to know my brothers. I think it sucks that you never told us about each other, and I won't let you keep us apart any longer."

"You've said your piece, now go," my father said, and promptly shut the door in our faces.

Fourteen

Mick

I watched the numbers go by as the elevator ascended.

After the faceoff with that douche-ass, Johnson, I'd brought Dru back to the hotel and left to go get dinner.

She seemed okay, but I wouldn't be surprised if she'd been holding it together for me, then lost her shit once I shut the door. Whether that meant crying out her frustrations or screaming them into a pillow, I didn't know, but I knew Dru was strong as hell and quite the bad-ass.

I grinned, thinking of her giving her father the business while he stood in front of her like he had a stick up his ass.

I didn't know why some men made amazing fathers, and others shouldn't be trusted caring for a hamster, but Dru and her sisters had definitely gotten the shit end of the stick when it came to fathers.

From everything I gathered, that's just the kind of deadbeat he was . . . his sons hadn't fared any better; in fact, they'd probably gotten it worse. Because, although I didn't think old Johnson had ever laid a hand on his girls, I had eye witnesses that said he hadn't been afraid to smack his boys around when they were young.

That shit probably stopped once they grew old enough to fight back. Lord knew there was no way Johnson was the kind of man who'd engage in a fair fight. He was the kind of scumbag who liked to pick on those he saw as weaker than he was.

Boy, I'd sure love to get him in the ring.

I stepped off the elevator, a large, steaming meat lover's pizza in one hand, and a cold six pack of beer in the other, and faltered.

Shit, what if Dru isn't the beer and pizza type?

Before I could second guess myself any further, the door two down from the elevator opened, and Dru's head popped out.

"Hey," she said with a small smile. "I was hoping it was you."

I searched her face as I moved toward her, noting a bit of puffiness, and shot her a smile of my own.

"I'd just realized I hadn't asked what you wanted when I left. I hope pizza and beer is okay. If not, I can run out and get wine and pasta, or some water and a sandwich . . . whatever you'd like."

Dru chuckled and stepped back to let me in to her room.

"Beer and pizza is perfect," she assured me, and I felt the knot in my belly loosen.

I didn't want to add to her shitty day. In fact, I'd do what I could to make her smile again, as much as possible.

I walked over to the small table in the corner and placed the pizza box on it, then pulled out a beer, popped the top, and handed it to her, before doing the same for myself.

Once we were seated in the chairs opposite each other, I asked, "How you holdin' up?"

Dru opened the lid of the pizza and selected a piece.

"A little disappointed, but overall okay." She shrugged. "I'm happy I got to tell him what I thought of him, and still in shock over the fact that we have three brothers. I hope Brody was serious about getting to know us."

"I'm sure he was," I assured her, even though I knew no such thing.

Still, if I found out I had three sisters, I sure as hell would want to get to know them.

Dru smiled and lifted the pizza to her lips. I tried not to stare at her mouth, so I shifted my focus to her hair. It was wet, so she must have showered while I was gone, and looked ink black. She had it pulled off of her face and piled on her head in a bun, which showcased her long neck.

Without realizing it, my gaze traveled down the length of her neck and settled on her cleavage.

Is it getting hot in here?

Shaking my head slightly, I turned my attention to the pizza, choosing my slice like it was a life or death decision, and took a long pull from my beer.

Once I'd selected the biggest, meatiest piece of pie, I cleared my throat and took a big bite. Only then did I look back into Dru's face, only to find her staring at me, a knowing grin tipping her lips up provocatively.

She'd totally busted me.

I shrugged, grinned, and demolished my slice.

"So, what about you, Mick? What are your parents like? You told me a little about your mom, but what about your dad?"

Pain sliced through my heart, like it always did when I thought of my pops, but being there with Dru when she confronted her father today, I didn't mind getting a little personal with her.

Plus, it was good to talk about him, to keep him at the forefront of my mind.

"My pops was the best," I told her, leaning back in my chair and balancing my beer on my knee. "He was a fighter, took me to the gym with him as a boy and taught me everything I know. He was a big brute, but the minute he laid eyes on my mother, he knew she was the one for him. They were good together. I can still hear the way they'd laugh with each other over breakfast each morning." I smiled, remembering the sound. The looks on both their faces. How happy they were. "But, fighting professionally ain't easy, especially back in those days, and he never made it big enough for the TV spots or the big paydays. Eventually, he had too many hits in the head, until the final blow killed him. He got knocked out and never got back up."

"Oh, my God, I'm so sorry," Dru said, reaching out and placing her hand on my knee, which was the closest thing to her. "How old were you?"

"Seventeen," I replied. "My parents met later in life, so got a later start at marriage and having me. I ended up being the only kid they could have, but I never minded. My ma never got over it, over *him* . . . never moved on or dated again, no matter how hard I tried to talk her into it. For her, he was it. *The one.*"

"My mom was the same way," Dru said softly. "Although, sounds like your mom won the lottery with your dad . . ."

She trailed off, and I knew she was thinking hers wasn't so lucky.

Fifteen

Dru

When I got back home from my trip, I went straight to work and didn't stop.

Not only were *both* my sisters enjoying their honeymoon, but I needed to keep my mind off of my trip to see our father. Tanisha, Claire, and the rest of the staff were fully capable of taking over Natasha and Millie's workloads, so it wasn't as if I had to stay late every night to cover the load of three people, but it felt good to escape into my work just the same.

I missed my sisters, and, yes, their husbands, too, and there was so much I wanted to tell them. On the trip back from Chicago, I'd decided to come clean about hiring Mick and going to see our dad. I was going to tell them everything, even if it meant dealing with their possible anger and or disappointment.

They deserved to know. And, once that chore was over, I was excited to tell them about our brothers.

Honestly, if the boys didn't exist, I might be able to keep finding our father a secret forever. But, I knew they'd want to learn we had brothers, to get the opportunity to meet them and hopefully grow some sort of relationship. But, I couldn't tell them about one without the other.

I also hadn't spoken to Mick since he'd dropped me off at home.

I'd thought about him constantly though. Not just because his mother's birthday party was coming up this weekend, and I'd been neck deep in planning it, but because that trip to Chicago had made me feel closer to him.

We never had talked about the kiss, but he'd shared so much about his past and his personal life, and I felt more than ever that I wanted to get to know him better.

The more I learned about Mick, the more I liked, and I found myself wanting to learn everything.

"Hey, you almost done?"

I looked up at smiled at Tanisha, before looking back down at my To-Do List and nodding.

"Yeah, just crossed the last thing off for today."

"Great . . . I was wondering if you'd maybe want to go grab a bite and a drink at Prime Beef. I called over and they have room at the bar."

I pushed back from my desk and stood, stretching my back out before replying, "That sounds great actually."

Much better than another night alone in front of the TV eating leftovers and drinking wine out of the bottle. Which may or may not have been the way I'd spent every other night this week.

"Do I have time to run upstairs and freshen up real quick? I won't take long, I promise."

"Yeah, I'll do the same and meet you in the hallway," Tanisha replied, and we walked out together, turning off lights as we walked.

Ten minutes later, I was showered, with my hair piled up in a bun and a comfy maxi dress on. I'd put on some light makeup, just because Prime Beef was the kind of place you went on a date, and called it good.

I was pretty sure they would have let me in even if I'd thrown on some sweat pants and a T-shirt and gone in bare-faced, what with Jericho being my brother-in-law and being on a first-name basis with most of the staff. But, that seemed not only rude, but like I was taking advantage; plus, I'd rather go into a place feeling comfortable, yet confident, rather than sloppy and like I'd just rolled out of bed.

Tanisha must have felt the same way, because she looked sweet and fresh herself, in a floral romper and gladiator sandals.

"Ready?" I asked.

"Am I ever," she replied with a light laugh, and we headed downstairs and across the street.

One of the best things about living above the shop was that fact that we were right in the middle of Main Street, and could walk to get just about any, and every thing. I loved the convenience of it, especially when I was busy at work.

"Hey, ladies, I saved a couple places for you at the bar after Tanisha called. You can go right on back," the pretty young hostess said after we walked in.

We thanked her and headed back to the bar.

I did my best to ignore the other patrons in the restaurant, not wanting to intrude on their happy moments or romantic glances. All I wanted was a fruity drink and some tasty appetizers, and I knew I was about to get both.

Tanisha and I got settled, ordered our drinks and began looking over the bar menu.

"Are you all set for Mrs. O'Donnelly's birthday party?"

"Oh, yeah, it's going to be so much fun. I cannot wait to meet

Mick's mom and see her face when she realizes what he's done for her. It's really the sweetest thing," I said, smiling down at my menu at the thought of Mick, and how cute he was every time he talked about his *ma*.

There was just something about a man who loved his mother . . . especially when he was a large, burly dude, who looked like he could bench press a semi.

"I read through the file when I was ordering the decorations, and I have to say, I think you've really outdone yourself with this one. We'll need to take tons of pictures, before and after, and get them up on our social media. I have a feeling this theme will be a big seller."

"Sounds good. I'll look in Tasha's file and get the number for the photographer," I said, then told the bartender, "I'd like the Ahi Poke Nachos, please," as he set my Moscow Mule in front of me.

"And, I'd like the Alaskan King Crab Cakes," Tanisha added, picking up her Lemon Drop martini and taking a sip.

"Thanks," I said, once the bartender walked away to input our order. "Admittedly I was one of the last on board with hiring staff and loosening the reigns on our baby, but we really hit the jackpot when we hired you, T."

"Well, well, two of the most beautiful women in the county have wandered into our restaurant . . ."

I looked over my shoulder and smiled at Hector.

"Just the county?" I asked, raising my eyebrow and biting back that smile.

"Sorry, I meant the country . . . Strike that, the *world*," he amended with a tip of his head.

"That's more like it," I said with a chuckle. "Hector, you know Tanisha, right?"

"Yes, we've met briefly," he said, moving past me to T and holding out his hand. "It's a pleasure to see you again."

I watched as she put her hand in his, then blush prettily when he raised it to his lips and kissed the back softly.

Hmmmm, interesting.

"Are you off? Would you care to join us?" I asked, thinking Tanisha may be just who Hector was looking for.

"Almost," he said, looking toward the kitchen and nodding, before adding, "Let me just finish a few things, then I'd love to join you for a drink."

When Hector walked away, Tanisha turned to me and said, "He is *so* hot . . . he makes me nervous."

"T, Hector *is* hot, but he's also the sweetest guy in the world. Plus, you are sitting there *on fire*, practically burning this place down. You have nothing to be nervous about. If you like him, show him. Go after what you want."

As soon as the words were out of my mouth, I knew I needed to take my own advice. The next time I saw Mick, I was not only going to bring up the kiss, but I was going to tell him how much I liked it, and why I thought we should do it again.

Repeatedly.

Sixteen

Mick

"All right, Ma, you're loaded up on Little Debbies, Jolly Ranchers, sweet tea, and I restocked the hot Funyons stash you didn't think I knew about."

My mother looked me straight in the eyes and didn't blink. Daring me to try and tell her what she could or couldn't eat.

I didn't have a death wish, so I let it pass.

"Now, let's get you dressed and I'll join you for dinner."

She narrowed her eyes at me, like I knew she would, and asked suspiciously, "What's wrong with what I'm wearing?"

I took in her bright-blue track suit and replied, "I just thought it would be nice for us to dress up a bit . . . have a nice dinner. It is your birthday, after all, and since you won't let me take you out, I'd like to join you here."

"No reason to go out and spend money on some fancy dinner just because I woke up a year older. You do look spiffy though, Mickie, I'll give you that . . . I just assumed it was for a lady friend," my ma said, then muttered, "Wishful thinking."

"I heard that," I said with a chuckle.

She shrugged, not the least bit worried. In her eyes, it was her duty to mention marriage and children *each and every* time I saw her. The older I got, the more often she slipped something about my bachelor status into conversation.

I didn't care, I knew she loved me and worried about me being alone.

I felt the same way about her.

"You know, I wouldn't be lonely if you'd move in with me," I tried.

Ma glared at me and said, "Get out my red dress. If my son's escorting me to dinner for my birthday, I guess I'll make an effort."

I turned before she could see my grin and went to the armoire to get out her favorite dress. Then I took out her dressy black flats, slip, and panty hose, and laid it all out for her.

"Here you go, I'll step out and give you some privacy."

I shut the door to my mom's room behind me and looked down the hall. Robert, the man my mom always accused of cheating at cards, and who I thought had a crush on her, was standing at the end of the hall. He was Dru's lookout.

I'd stopped in earlier to see how the setup was going, and I could already tell that Dru had outdone herself on planning my mom's party.

The rec room was decked out in red and black. There were tables set up for roulette, craps, black jack, and poker, as well as keno in the corner. There was a huge tiered birthday cake, also red and black, with an ace, spade, club, and heart, surrounding the large letters that said, *Happy Eighty-Fifth Birthday, Dotty.*

I held up my hands, indicating we'd be ready in ten minutes, and Robert hurried off to go tell Dru.

He was taking his duties as lookout very seriously.

Ten minutes later, my ma was ready, and we were walking through the halls, her hand in my arm.

"Where you goin'? The cafeteria is at the end of the hall, you know that," Ma said when I turned toward the rec room.

"I just wanted to check on Robert real quick and he said he'd be in the rec room," I fibbed.

Ma rolled her eyes.

"Is it Robert's birthday, or mine? I'm hungry."

"It'll just take a minute," I assured her, then pushed opened the door and led her inside.

"Oh my . . . what is all this?" Ma asked softly, her hand tightening on my arm as she took in the room.

Everyone was there, waiting to yell, "Happy Birthday," and I noticed my ma's eyes getting wet as she took in the rec room-turned-casino.

I fished the handkerchief out of my pocket and handed it to her.

"Happy Birthday, Ma," I whispered, dropping a kiss on her cheek.

"Oh, Mickie, it's too much."

I looked down into her beautiful face and replied, "Never enough."

She patted my arm and gave me a watery smile, then turned to the room and yelled, "Get ready to lose! Mickie, take me to the black jack table . . . and get me some of that good food I smell."

"Yes, ma'am," I replied, then shot Dru a grateful grin.

Once my mom was happily deposited at her table, I walked over to where Dru was standing by the buffet line.

"This is perfect, thank you," I said as I grabbed my mom a plate.

"She looked surprised, and very happy. Good job, Mick," Dru replied sweetly, and I took a second to take her in.

She was dressed for business in her pants suit, but her floral blouse and loose curls softened the look up and made her look classy, yet touchable. And I had the sudden urge to touch her.

I cleared my throat and got back to the business of getting my mom's dinner.

"She deserves a special day. My dad always made a big deal out of her birthday, and since he's been gone, I've been lucky if she lets me get her a present and wish her happy birthday. She just hasn't wanted to celebrate without him, ya know. But, I couldn't let her eighty-fifth go by like that, and, after seeing her face tonight, I'm going to make sure every birthday from now on is a big deal. My dad would want that."

I felt Dru's hand on my arm, and when I looked in her face, I saw the yearning there. It was the same yearning I felt whenever I was around her.

"I'd better take this to Ma, don't want her getting hangry at her own party," I said, suddenly feeling like a big-ass chicken.

Dru smiled indulgently, not fooled by my excuse.

"Okay, but Mick, we will talk . . . *tonight*."

I nodded, then stalked off, wondering how I was going to let her down again, or if I even wanted to.

Seventeen

Dru

I indulged myself by watching Mick walk away for a moment, then bit back my smile and got back to work.

My stomach was a mess of nerves, but I felt hopeful.

Mick didn't seem to be as resolved to holding me at arm's length. Not that I was trying to force him into liking me, *but,* since I was pretty sure he already did, I didn't feel bad about forcing his hand a little.

I was a strong, independent woman, who knew her own mind and what she wanted. And it was time for me to take my own advice and go after it.

"How's everything going? We still good on everything?" I asked Claire.

She looked down at the clipboard in her hand and said, "So far, so good. The guests really like the meatballs, spring rolls, and roast beef, but I don't think we'll run out."

"Great, I'm going to walk the room."

I made my way around the rec room, checking with the staff to make sure they were all right, and making the room looked up to snuff. I had a big smile on my face as I took it all in, inordinately pleased with how the event had turned out.

Well, at least as far as décor and guest involvement. We wouldn't know for sure if it was a success until it was over, but, barring anything crazy happening, I thought this would definitely be the benchmark for any casino parties to come.

I was gathering thoughts for my After Action Report as I checked in on the gaming tables, then stopped when I saw Mick's mother get up from the black jack table and start moving toward the poker table.

I didn't see Mick, so I hurried over to help her.

"Mrs. O'Donnelly," I called, coming up beside her and offering my arm. "I was hoping to get the chance to meet you and say happy birthday," I added easily, helping her cross the room. "I'm Druscilla, Dru. Your son hired me for this party."

She grinned up at me, looking so much like her son my heart warmed.

"You did all this?" she asked, gesturing to the room with her free hand.

"Yes, ma'am."

"Ma'am? Oh, no, I don't have one foot in the grave yet . . . call me Dottie."

I let out a small laugh and amended, "Yes, Dottie, I did this, but it was all Mick's idea."

Just then, I saw him. He was standing next to a much smaller, much older gentleman, his face full of mirth as they talked.

I felt that now-familiar flutter when he raised his glass of sweet tea with fresh peaches at me.

I smiled back at him, then let out a soothing breathe as I tried to calm my racing heart.

Can I really do it? Put myself out there and possibly face rejection again? If he didn't want me after I put myself out there, and after that kiss, that would be it. I'd accept his wishes and walk away.

"How did you say you knew Mickie again?"

I blinked, bringing myself out of my thoughts as we reached an open chair at the poker table.

"Oh, well, initially we met through his friend Jackson, who just got married to my sister, Millie. And, he's also friends with Jericho, who is married to my other sister, Natasha. But, I recently got to know him better when I hired him."

"Are you married?" Dottie asked as she eased into the seat.

"No, I'm single," I replied, and I could have sworn, I saw her eyes light up.

"And what do you think of Mickie? He's handsome, makes a good living, has his own home . . ."

I couldn't help but laugh as she listed Mick's attributes.

"Mick's a great guy," I assured her. "You did a wonderful job with him. But, he has a policy about dating clients."

"Oh, is he currently doing an investigation for you? When will it be resolved?"

Dottie picked up her cards and looked at them, then took out three and tossed them toward the dealer, before placing the remaining two face down in front of her.

"Well, no, actually, I guess his job for me is technically done . . . all we have left is his final report and my last payment."

"Well, then, I guess his policy no longer applies, now does it?" she asked, her eyes on the cards.

Even though she wasn't facing me, I could tell her lips were turned up.

"No, I would think that it doesn't. Although, I'm not sure Mick will see it that way," I replied softly.

"Then, make him see it," Dottie said, her voice strong and sure.

"Yes, ma'am," I said, chuckling when she let out a huff. "Is there anything I can get for you?"

"All I want for my birthday is my son's happiness."

Wow, she's good, I thought as I left her to continue my rounds.

After a couple hours of gambling, eating, and talking a whole lot of smack to each other, the residents of Dottie's home, and the birthday girl herself, were clearly exhausted. Guests started to go to their rooms, some stopping to thank us for the party, others simply disappearing with fists full of play money, which the facility had provided.

"I'm gonna take Mom to her room, then I'll be back to help," Mick said, coming up behind me.

I turned from where I'd been boxing leftover food for the guests and said, "Oh, I'd like to say goodnight, if she's not too tired."

"Ma'd kill me if I ever said she was too tired for anything, let alone the chance to thank you for making her birthday party perfect."

We walked over to Dottie, who was watching us with a look of unadulterated hope, and I felt a tug of happiness because she obviously liked me for her son.

"Dottie, I hope you had a wonderful birthday. Thank you so much for letting us share it with you," I said, holding out my hand.

She looked at my hand and gave a *pshhh* sound, then held out her arms and said, "Bring it in."

I heard Mick's chuckle as I leaned down to give her a quick, *soft*, hug. Although she was tough in spirit, her body felt slight, fragile, so I took care as I held her briefly.

"I'll be back," Mick said as he turned his mother toward the door.

As they walked away, I heard Dottie say, "Son, if you have a brain in your head, you won't let that one get away. Smart, pretty, and successful? Girls like that don't come around often. I'd like some grandchildren before I die . . ."

I got back to work with a smile, as I heard Mick grumble in response.

Eighteen

Mick

After getting an earful from Ma about Dru while she got ready for bed, I'd finally gotten her settled and was headed back to the rec room to see if I could help with tear down.

Ma was still feeling the adrenaline rush from her party, and I wasn't sure if she was gonna crash or stay up half the night reading. Or, more likely, stay up half the night plotting out my future with Dru, who she'd somehow managed to fall in love with and mentally marry me off to, after a fifteen-minute conversation.

When I stepped into the room, I was surprised to see that it was almost completely set back to rights. Dru's crew were working methodically, loading their things up in bins and on carts, while others were putting the room back the way it had been.

"Wow, you guys work fast," I said as I approached Dru.

She smiled over her shoulder and replied, "Most of them have been with us for six months or more, so they're used to the routine. Tearing down is a lot easier than setting up, and everyone usually gets their second wind when they know it's almost time to go home."

"Makes sense. So, *ah*, do you still want to talk tonight, or are you too tired?" I asked, not sure if I was hoping she'd say yes or no.

It wasn't that I was afraid to talk to her, or that I didn't enjoy the hell out of spending time with her. I just didn't want to disappoint her again.

"Yes, I'd still like to talk, if *you're* not too tired," Dru replied.

I shook my head.

"I'm good. You wanna head out for a drink?"

"It's been a long day; would you mind coming to my place instead? I live in an apartment above Three Sisters," she asked, and my body tightened at the thought of being alone with her in her place.

Not that I was an animal or anything . . . I could control my urges, but I knew it would be much easier to keep my hands, and lips, to myself in a public place.

Still, she looked so hopeful, I said, "Sure, I can stop on the way and pick up some beer."

"Great, that gives me time to get things settled with work. I do have some whiskey and maybe a bottle of wine or two, but Jericho finished off the beer last time he and Tasha were over."

"It's no problem, I'll pick some up," I assured her, then added, "Well, if you don't need me, I'll meet you at your place in, what, thirty?"

"Sounds good," Dru said with a smile, then turned back to her work.

I thanked the admin at the front desk again for allowing us to take over for my ma's birthday, then got in my Jeep and headed toward the nearest convenience store.

I wandered the aisles, thinking about Dru. I'd gotten to know her a lot in the weeks I'd been working for her.

It's funny how you can go from not knowing someone, to them

becoming a part of your everyday life. The difference was, with most of my previous clients, once their cases were closed, I no longer spoke, or saw, them, unless they hired me again.

That hadn't been the case with Jackson or Jericho. They'd somehow gone from clients to friends, and were now two of the most important people in my life. With Dru, it looked to be going the same way. The fact that those friends were now also her family, made a relationship with Dru seem even more likely.

But, what kind of relationship do I want with her?

I was attracted to her. We had chemistry, *the kiss had solidified that fact,* and I liked spending time with her. But, other than sharing friends, and having that sexual attraction, what did we really have in common?

I looked at my watch and grabbed a six pack, thinking Dru should be almost done, and moved toward the counter to check out.

When I pulled in behind Three Sisters Catering, I saw the last few employees getting in their cars, and Claire turning off the lights in the building. I'd only seen Claire in passing, but knew from hearing Millie talk that she was her right hand in the kitchen.

I beeped my alarm and cleared my throat as I walked, wanting to be loud enough for her to hear me and hopefully not freak her out. I was a big dude, the kind a woman wouldn't feel comfortable running into at night, if she didn't know me.

When she turned her head, I lifted a hand and said, "Hey, Claire, I'm Mick. I'm here to see Dru."

"Oh, hey, Mick," she replied, the relief in her voice evident. "You just go in through there and up the stairs."

"Thanks, have a good night. Drive safe."

I looked around the parking lot. It was to the side of the building, not behind, so you could see Main Street, and not only was the street lit up, but they had lights in the back of the building as well, so the lot was well-lit.

"I will, thanks. Oh, and, Mick, I have to say, I love your mother. She's hilarious. I really think she had a great time tonight."

I couldn't help but grin. Ma had always had that *thing* about her that made people like her and want to be around her.

"She did, and it was all thanks to you and your crew. I appreciate all the hard work you all put into making tonight special."

Claire nodded and said, "Of course, it was our pleasure."

I waited until she was safely in her car and pulling out of the lot, before I went inside and up the stairs.

When I got to the top and saw there were actually four apartments, I pulled out my phone to call Dru and ask which was hers, then realized one of the doors in the middle was open. I kept going down the hall, hoping it was hers and she'd left it open for me, rather than some stranger who would probably freak if I darkened their doorway.

I peered around the corner, then leaned against the doorway with a grin, while I watched Dru dash around her apartment, trying to clean things up.

Nineteen

Dru

Gah, what had I been thinking? Why didn't I invite him over once I knew my apartment was clean?

I'd walked in to my apartment, excited that Mick was coming over, then I'd looked around and realized my slob was on display.

The place wasn't dirty . . . I always did my dishes, vacuumed, and made sure my apartment was *clean*, but I was a messy person. Always had been. That meant, that although my laundry *was* clean, it was strewn about my living room from when I'd been looking for my favorite pajama shirt last night, and T-back bra this morning.

I'd hurried in and began running around the living room, picking up clothes and shoving them back into the laundry basket.

I ran into my room, threw the full basket on my unmade bed, and hurried back out to see what else needed to be put away. That's when I saw Mick standing just inside my doorway, a sexy grin on his lips.

"Oh, hey," I managed between pants. "How long have you been standing there?"

I moved toward him and took the six pack of beer out of his hands, then went into the kitchen and set it on the counter.

"Long enough," he replied with a chuckle, causing me to flush.

"So, you know my big secret . . . I'm a bit of a slob," I admitted, pulling out two bottles of beer and popping the tops off, before handing one to Mick.

"If that's your biggest flaw, then I have to say, you're damn near perfect."

I looked into his light-green eyes, saw the sincerity there, and asked, "Will you go out with me? To dinner . . . on a date?"

My nerves were humming with pleasure from his compliment and worry over his answer, so I took a long drink of the cold beer and waited to hear what he'd say.

"Dru . . ." Mick began, like he was gonna argue his no-client rule again, so I figured I'd better lay it all out on the line before he could deny me again.

"I'm no longer your client, not really. I mean, you found my dad, I talked to him. Case closed. All we have to do is wrap it up and call it good. I don't think I'll ever need a PI again, so you can just take me off your client list and we can give this a shot . . . What do you say?"

"You've really been thinking about this . . ."

Did that mean he hadn't been?

Worried that he was going to come to a snap decision again, I decided it was time for a little distraction.

"Are you hungry? I have some leftovers Millie left for me. I didn't really eat much today."

"If you're having some, sure, I can always eat," Mick replied as I took containers out of the fridge. "Do you cook?"

I looked up at him briefly as I made us each a plate.

"Yes, actually, I do. I know Millie's the chef in the family, but our mom taught us all to cook. In fact, when we were little, she would put us in charge of a special night. So, say it was Valentine's Day, and it was my turn to cook, I would have to make up a menu, find recipes, and go shopping with her for ingredients, then she'd help make the dinner that night. At first, we were annoyed by it, well, Tasha and I were, Millie always loved it, but, as I got older, those became my favorite days. When it was just me and mom putting together out dinner for the night."

I lifted the cartons as I put them back in the fridge.

"Millie just made me these because she knew I'd be putting in a lot of hours, with both her and Tasha gone, and she wanted to make sure I was eating a proper meal."

"Sounds like you and your sisters are all pretty tight. With each other, and with your ma."

"Yeah, we are. We all miss her . . . It's nice that we have each other to take care of."

Once I'd heated up our food, we took it to my small square dining room table, and settled in.

"So, what do you say . . . You, me . . . dinner?" I said again, once he was relaxed with his food and drink.

Mick grinned at me and asked, "Do you think we'd be a good fit?"

I nodded eagerly.

"*Yes,*" I practically shouted. "Don't tell me you've forgotten that kiss. I mean, did you black out? Think it was a dream? Have an out-of body-experience? We are definitely well-suited."

He chuckled.

"Yeah, I was there, and I definitely remember. But, although chemistry is necessary, it isn't everything. Do you think we have enough in common, in other areas? I mean, I'm an Irish brute, who sometimes deals with lowlifes and solves problems with my fists . . . You're an amazingly smart and sexy as hell woman, and have more class in your little finger than I have in my whole body. I'm beer and pizza and your champagne and caviar . . ."

I looked at him sharply, ignoring the happy beating of my heart over the way he saw me.

"I hope you're not trying to insinuate that you're not good enough for me, or that I'm somehow *better* than you, because that's insulting to us both," I said, practically baring my teeth when he grinned. "And, for the record, I hate caviar and love pizza . . ."

Mick chuckled and held up his hands.

"Sorry, I didn't mean to offend, I just want you to know what you're getting into. It's not all finding lost fathers and nights at the bar with our friends . . . You've met my ma, well, I try and spend time with her every day. She won't let me move her in with me, but I hate the thought of her being lonely in that place, even if it's where she wants to be. Some women I've dated have found it hard sharing me and my time with my ma."

"Those women are assholes," I said back without thinking. "I'd give anything to be able to see my mom every day, and there's no way I'd begrudge you spending time with yours. As for the rest of it, that's what dating is, right? Getting to know each other? All I'm asking for is the chance to get to know you." A thought hit me and I reached out to take his hand. "What if we did *a day in the life?*"

"What's that?"

"Monday's my next day off. What if on Monday I spend the whole day with you, as your shadow, so to speak, to see how you live your life day to day. Then, whenever you have a free day, you can shadow me. This will give us a more in-depth view of what makes each other tick. Kind of a crash course in getting to know each other."

"Sounds weird. Have you done this before?"

"No, I saw it on TV. It was actually about people shadowing other people to see if they'd be a good fit for a job, but I thought it sounded cool and would work for relationships, too," I admitted. "Not only would it give us more one on one time together, and let us learn more about each other, it would let us see how we would fit into each other's lives. Then, once we've both done our shadow days, you can let me know if you'll accept my invitation to dinner or not."

"You're serious?" he asked.

"Completely. I like you, Mick, and I'm willing to do whatever it takes to show you that we should do this thing. What do you say?"

"I say, *all right*. Let's do the thing."

Twenty

Mick

It was four forty-five in the morning when I pulled up outside Three Sisters fully expecting to have to wait for Dru, or possibly wake her up. Instead, she was waiting outside, chipper and bouncing on her heels in excitement.

Fuck, she looks great.

In yoga pants and a tank top that showcased her curves and left nothing to the imagination, with her hair pulled back into a ponytail and her face devoid of makeup, Dru was absolutely stunning.

Before I could open the door to my Jeep and go around to help her in, she was already seated with her seatbelt on, her face turned toward me with a smile.

"Good morning!"

Now, I got up this early because it was my routine, and the only time I could fit in my workout. That didn't mean I liked it, nor was I used to being met with a ray of sunshine before the sun had even come up.

Still, I couldn't help but grin in the face of Dru's exuberance.

"Morning," I replied, my voice still gruff with sleep. "You ready?"

"So ready. I barely slept, I was so nervous and excited," she admitted, laying it all out with absolutely no guile.

I liked that.

"I hope you got enough to make it through the day, cause it's gonna be a long one," I warned.

"Aye, aye, Captain," Dru replied saucily, turning back so she was sitting right in her seat as I took off toward the gym.

I chuckled, and we spent the rest of the trip in relative silence, with the tunes of Pink Floyd filling the void.

We parked and walked inside, and I cannot lie, I enjoyed the view of her ass in those yoga pants. So much so, that I had to think of the time I saw a man masturbate with an orange when I was on a case.

That always did the trick.

By the time I showed her where the women's locker room was, my body was back to normal and I'd made a vow not to look below her neck until she was changed for the day and out of those pants.

We put our things up in our respective locker rooms, then met back out in the common area.

"I usually warm up, sometimes run or do some lifting, then spar. You can use whatever you'd like . . . I'll give you a heads up when I'm going to shower."

"When you say spar, do you mean you're going to fight someone up there in the ring?" she asked, her eyes wide.

"Yeah, I mean, it won't be as serious as if we were actually fighting, but we'll be throwing punches."

"Oh . . . can I watch?"

"Sure, if you want. I'll let you know when it's my turn."

Dru nodded, then left me to go get on the treadmill, while I went to the mats and started stretching out. Once I was done with that I did some work on the speedbag, and then the punching bag.

An hour later, I caught Dru's eye and lifted my chin toward the mat. It was time for my sparring session.

I peeled off my sweaty shirt, wiped myself off with my towel, and held out my hands to get them taped up. Once I was ready, I stepped into the ring and hit gloves with Tank, one of the professional fighters at the gym.

He and I often sparred together, since we were in the same weight class.

I was so focused on what I was doing, which was important if I didn't want to get my ass kicked, that I didn't remember that Dru had been watching until I ducked under the ropes and hopped down onto the floor.

I took a long drink from my water bottle, wiped the sweat from my face, and turned to see her standing behind me, kind of glassy eyed.

"What'd you think?" I asked.

Without warning, Dru stepped up to me and reached up to cup my face and bring it down, meeting my lips with hers.

With my adrenaline pumping and the woman who'd been keeping me awake at night in my arms, I responded with fervor, my hands going down to cup the ass I'd been appreciating all morning.

After a few heated moments, I became aware of a high whistle and pulled back, panting out breaths as I looked up to find the coach watching us with a scowl.

"Not in my gym, O'Donnelly," he said gruffly, then turned his attention back to the boxers in the ring.

"Sorry," Dru said, pulling my attention away from Coach and back to her blushing face.

"Never apologize for a kiss like that," I said with a grin, letting her go before we got reprimanded again and I got on Coach's bad side.

She smiled, cheeks still blazing, and took a step back.

I tried not to notice her breasts heaving with each heavy breath, and failed. *So much for not looking below her neck.*

"What do you say we go get cleaned up, then I'll take you to breakfast?"

"Sounds perfect," Dru said, then turned and headed toward the lady's locker room.

I took a moment to finish my water and watch her walk away, before turning toward the men's locker room.

I needed a cold shower.

Twenty-One

Dru

I stayed under the cold spray until my lips were quivering, but I still couldn't get the sight of Mick's muscles out of my head.

When he'd taken off his shirt and got up into the ring, I'd felt like one of those cartoon characters with their tongue hanging out, that had to be rolled back up and into their mouths. Then he'd started to move, and the way his muscles had bunched and bulged was enough to make this independent business woman swoon like it was eighteenth-century England.

I'd never been someone who watched MMA fights or boxing. I wasn't a fan of violence or people getting physical when they got angry, but after a few minutes of watching Mick, I knew I'd had it all wrong.

It was beautiful.

He was beautiful.

Mick had told me his father had been a professional fighter, and although I didn't think *he* ever had, Mick had obviously put in a lot of work and training. He was full of grace and precision, and watching him up there had done things to my libido I hadn't known was possible.

I don't know if I could handle watching him in a professional fight, where he and another man were trying to annihilate each other, but I could watch him spar *all day*.

This kiss had been pure instinct. Driven by lust and the need to put my hands all over his body. The timing and location sucked, but keeping my hands to myself was out of the question.

I was a little calmer now that I'd frozen the hormones right out of my body, and I was pretty sure I could get through the rest of the day without attacking him again. Unless he got into a random sparring match during the course of business . . . then, all bets were off.

Mick had said to dress casually, so I'd brought jeans and a pretty blouse to wear for the rest of the day.

"Hey, you ready?" Mick asked when I came out of the locker room.

"Yes, I'm starving."

"Let's go feed you then."

Ten minutes later, we were seated at a small diner near his office, with a pretty older waitress wearing her hair up in a bun with bright-red lipstick serving up coffee.

"I'll have four eggs over medium, the roasted potatoes, bacon, and a side of fruit," Mick said, and I felt my eyes widen at his order.

But, I guess when you had a body like his to maintain, you needed all the fuel you could get.

"Can I have the Greek omelet, please?"

"Coming right up," the server said, then left us with our full cups of coffee.

"So, how are the honeymooners doing?" Mick asked, taking a sip from his black coffee, while I added cream to mine.

"Tasha and Jericho still have a week in Bali, so I'm sure they're doing fantastic. The last pictures she sent were from some kind of monkey sanctuary, or forest . . . I don't know, but she had a monkey on her shoulder and looked like she was freaking out."

Mick chuckled and asked, "And Jackson and Millie?"

"They actually got back in last night."

"If you need to take a break from the day to go see them, I totally understand."

"Oh, no, you're not getting rid of me that easily," I said with a laugh. "I'm sure they're exhausted, and want to spend the day with Kayla. Tomorrow will be soon enough for me to stop in and hear all about their trip."

Mick nodded.

I leaned forward on the table and asked, "So, what else is on the agenda? Are we going after any bad guys?"

"Sorry, nothing that exciting," Mick replied with a grin. "We'll go by the office, see if I have any new calls or updates on current cases, do some admin, then stop by the grocery store and pick up stuff for Ma. When I told her you'd be with me, she asked me to pick up sandwich stuff so we could have lunch with her, I hope that's all right."

"Yes, of course it is. I like Dottie a lot. She's hilarious," I replied, excited at the thought of seeing Mick's mom again.

"I don't know how hilarious you'll find her when you realize her current goal in life is to see us matched up."

I looked into his beautiful eyes, trying to decipher whether or not *he* minded her plotting to get us together. By the way they were crinkled up at the sides, I didn't think he minded too much.

Hopefully that meant he was finally giving up the resistance and willing to give us a shot.

"I'm sure I won't mind," I said softly.

Mick opened his mouth to respond, but when our server dropped our plates in front of us, he looked at her and said, "Thanks."

I gave a little internal sigh, but thought, *It's okay, we have all day and I'm not giving up.*

"This looks great," I added, placing my napkin on my lap as I got ready to dig into my omelet.

"Yeah, as I was saying, after we leave my ma's, I have to do some recon for a client. He says his ex stole their dog, so we'll see if we can spot the pup and get some pictures of the dog and the ex together."

"Oh, cool, you mean we might get to do a stakeout?"

Mick looked like he was holding back a smile when he replied, "It'll probably be as easy as looking in the backyard, but maybe you'll get your wish and we can sit in the Jeep in front of the house for a few hours."

"Goody," I said, clapping my hands together before picking up my fork. "I can't wait."

Mick chuckled again, making my insides quiver and my hormones unthaw.

Little did he know, if I got what *I* wanted, this *day in the life* would transition into a *night in the life* . . .

Twenty-Two

Mick

I looked up and over my computer screen to see Dru studying my record collection, her pointer finger moving over each spine as she read the titles.

Honestly, I thought she'd be bored to death by now, but as soon as we'd arrived at my office, she'd volunteered to check the messages on what she called my *Jurassic answering machine,* as well as my voicemail on my cell, and write down any pertinent information. This freed me up to work on my report for a client whose case I'd just finished.

By the time the report was done and emailed, she'd completed the transcription and handed off the information to me, so I could call back those I needed to.

Now I was just finishing up some email correspondence and ensuring I had everything for our case later in the day, and Dru had busied herself by checking out my office, commenting as she explored.

"This leather is so comfortable."

"What kind of stuff do you have recorded on your DVR?"

"Ohhh, I love this Beatles album."

Surprisingly, her commentary wasn't distracting; instead I found that I liked having her in the office while I worked. Her presence was soothing, and I loved to listen to her talk, even if she was mostly just muttering to herself.

I was in danger of becoming addicted to Dru and we hadn't really even begun yet.

"You ready to head out?" I asked, logging off my computer.

"Yup."

We loaded up in the Jeep after I locked up my office, stopping at the local market to pick up Ma's grocery items before heading to her assisted living facility.

Once we were there, I knocked lightly on the door before opening it and announcing we were there.

"Druscilla, come in dear," Dottie said as we stepped inside.

She was sitting in her chair watching a courtroom show, but I noticed that her hair was done and she was dressed.

"Hello, Dottie, it's so good to see you again," Dru said, crossing to give my ma a hug.

"You look lovely," Ma said, her weathered face beaming.

"Thank you, so do you."

"Hi, Ma, it's me, your dutiful son . . . What, no greeting?" I asked jokingly, secretly pleased that she liked Dru so much.

Although, I guess it had been years since I'd brought a woman I was dating to meet her, so it wasn't surprising that she was holding on to the possibility of Dru and I dating with both hands.

"Pshhh, I see you every day," Ma retorted. "Let me enjoy some girl time."

I shook my head, but left them be and went to her small kitchen to set out the sandwich stuff and chips, and put everything else away.

"Want me to make the sandwiches?" I asked when I was done.

"Yes, Mickie," Ma said, waving her hand at me dismissively, too intent on her conversation with Dru.

"I'd ask what you want on it, but don't want to get my head bit off," I muttered to myself as I put together the turkey sandwiches.

I placed the three plates of sandwiches, a big back of chips, and three waters on the table, then looked over at Ma and Dru to see them still leaned in close, talking softly and smiling like long-lost friends.

"Lunch is ready," I announced, then went over to help Ma out of the chair and to the table.

Once we were all seated, I opened the bag of chips, then looked up to see them both watching me.

"What?" I asked.

"Thanks for lunch," Dru said.

"Did you get my hot Funyons?" Ma asked.

"Yeah, Ma, I did, but I gotta say, I don't think those are good for you."

"I've lived long enough to know my own mind, haven't I? I think I should be able to eat what I want," Ma countered.

"I agree," I replied, then added, "Within reason." Ma pursed her lips. "You need to mind your health and burning your gut with some dyed, processed, powdered junk food cannot possibly be healthy."

"Not all of us are health nuts like you and your pop . . . and, don't forget, I breast fed you, potty trained you, dealt with you during puberty and your hulk-like growth years. I lived most of my life for you and your father, shouldn't I get to live for me now?"

"Jeez, Ma, *yes*, if the hot Funyons mean that much to you, for God's sake, eat 'em."

"Don't you take the Lord's name in front of me."

It took every ounce of willpower I had not to roll my eyes.

"Sorry," I managed, then stuffed my mouth with sandwich before anything else accidently flew out.

I scowled when I noticed my mom shaking her head and Dru trying not to laugh.

"Dru, can you be a dear and go get me my Funyons?" Ma asked, shooting me a look that dared me to object.

I sighed as Dru said, "Of course," and pushed back from the table.

Once she was gone, my Ma leaned in and whispered, "If you let that one go, you're out of my will."

Nice, Ma . . .

Twenty-Three

Dru

"There she is!" I squealed, then clasped my hand over my mouth.

Not that the lady currently walking down her front steps, dog leash in hand, could've heard me from inside Mick's Jeep two blocks away, but . . . still. We were on a stakeout and I didn't want to raise suspicion.

Mick's laughter drifted through the cab and I turned to him, wide-eyed, then dropped my hand and mouthed, *sorry.*

"It's okay, I don't think she heard you," he replied good-naturedly, then lifted the long lens of his professional camera and pointed it out the dashboard toward where the tall raven-haired woman was waiting while her schnauzer went to the bathroom on her neighbor's lawn.

I watched the woman carefully, half expecting her to realize we were watching her, and why, and bolt.

Instead, she let her dog do its business and continued on their walk.

"Huh," I said, feeling a little let down by the lack of drama and suspense.

"Kind of anticlimactic?" Mick asked, not lowering his lens as he snapped pictures repeatedly.

"No . . . I don't know . . . Okay, maybe a little," I admitted, turning to look at him in my seat. "I would have liked to get out and chase someone, although, after the workout this morning, I probably wouldn't have gotten very far."

"I'm sure you would have done great. But, in all honesty, my job really isn't like that. I let the police handle the dangerous cases and any pursuits of criminals. Most of my cases deal with people trying to track someone down, like you, Jackson, and Jericho, or people trying to find out if their significant other is cheating, or get dirt on an ex . . . stuff like that."

"Oh, that makes sense. I'd hate to think of you putting yourself in dangerous situations."

"Hope you're not disappointed," Mick said, lowering his camera and taking it apart so he could put it back in its case.

"Not at all. I had a lot of fun today," I replied, reaching out to touch his forearm. "Thanks for agreeing to my crazy idea."

"I've had fun, too," Mick admitted with a wry grin. "So, did you have any thoughts about dinner?"

I let out a laugh.

"I feel like half the day was spent either planning our next meal, or eating it. I usually don't think about eating until my stomach starts growling and I realize I haven't eaten all day."

"Talking about, and eating, food is one of my favorite pastimes. There's no way I'd ever forget to eat. That's madness," Mick said, starting up the Jeep and pulling away from the curb. "Do you like Chinese food?"

"I do."

"What do you say we pick some up and take it back to my place?"

"Your house?" I asked.

"Yeah, my house. I don't live at the office. At least, I try not to."

"That sounds perfect. I'd love to see where you live," I said, thinking this day had turned out even better than I'd imagine when I suggested it.

"All right then."

We stopped and picked up Chinese food and drove to Mick's house, which was a sweet little ranch-style house located in between his office and his mom's home.

As we walked inside, I looked everywhere, trying to take it all in at once. His home was neat and clean, much more so than mine had been, and the living room furnishings were pretty minimal. There weren't a lot of things adorning the walls, or trinkets filling the shelves. He had more records filling his shelves, along with a record player and a few small instruments on display. There was also a guitar in a stand next to the fireplace and the biggest television I'd ever seen taking up one whole wall.

His furnishings were built for comfort, with deep lush cushions, and the recliner next to the sectional was obviously where he spent most of his time. It was facing the TV, with a large remote propped on the arm of the chair, and an end table next to it.

The room screamed *bachelor* with its lack of frills and throw pillows, but the dark-blue hues made it feel very homey.

I wanted to lay down on that couch with a fuzzy blanket and take a nap, although I doubted Mick would touch a fuzzy blanket with a ten-foot pole.

"Do you play?" I asked him, gesturing at the guitar.

"No," he replied with a shake of his head. "I just like to pick up collector items now and then. That one's signed by *The Rolling Stones*." Mick looked at the guitar like some women looked at diamonds, then said, "Come back to the kitchen and we'll get the food sorted."

I followed him out of the living room, through the dining room, which had a gorgeous, large sturdy wood table that looked like a large tree had been sliced in half and polished up, and into the kitchen.

"This is nice," I said as we stepped into the renovated space. "And, I have to say, that dining room table is amazing."

"Thanks, I have a friend who makes 'em," Mick said as he set the white containers on the granite countertop of the island. "And, I just finished the kitchen last summer. I'm pretty happy about how it turned out."

"You mean, you did this? Yourself?" I asked, incredulous.

I looked at the pretty countertops, the slate-gray cabinets, and shining stainless steel appliances.

"Yup, it was kind of a passion project," Mick said with a half shrug as he dished up the food.

"Wow, it's beautiful. It's the kind of kitchen that makes you long for a bunch of people to come over, so you can cook all the things."

"Yeah, I've been meaning to invite everyone over, it's just been so busy there never seems to be time."

"You should," I exclaimed, wondering if he'd let me use that oven. "When Tasha and Jericho get back, things will settle down. I'm sure everyone would love to come over and hang out, see where you live."

He nodded and handed me a plate.

"Wanna eat at the table, or watch something on TV?" he asked.

I thought about it for a minute, struggling to decide between that table and that big screen.

"TV," I replied. "We can sit at the table for breakfast."

I didn't bother hiding my grin as I took the plate and sashayed out of the room, ignoring the shock on Mick's face.

Twenty-Four

Mick

After Dru walked out, I lifted my jaw up off the floor and followed her.

You had to love a woman who wasn't afraid to ask for what she wanted. And, since the day we met, Dru had made it apparent that what she wanted was . . . *me*.

I wasn't sure if I was flattered or terrified. Maybe a bit of both.

Dru was sitting on the couch, feet up and tucked in to her side, her plate on the end table next to her.

"Do you have a throw?" she asked.

I looked at her, puzzled.

"A what?"

"A throw . . . you know, a blanket."

"Uh, I've never heard a blanket called that, but . . . the only blanket I have is the comforter on my bed. Do you want that?" I asked.

I mean, my mom kept a blanket on her chair at her place, but that's because she's older and always cold, I didn't realize it was a thing most people did, cover up while sitting around watching TV.

Is that even comfortable when wearing jeans?

When I covered myself up, that meant I was going to sleep.

I didn't get it . . .

"No," Dru replied with a laugh. "You don't have to mess up your bed. I'm fine."

"Are you sure? Cause I'll get it."

"I'm sure, don't worry about it."

She picked up her plate and dug in to her beef and broccoli, while I looked around the room and wondered what she thought of my place.

I'd never really worried about it before. Not that I'd brought a ton of women back here, maybe one or two over the years, but I'd never been serious about any of them, so whether they liked my house or not was irrelevant.

But, with Dru, it was different.

I want her to feel comfortable here, I realized. *To want to come back again, and again.*

I cleared my throat, surprised by my thoughts, and picked up the remote.

"What do you want to watch?" I asked as I pulled up the guide.

"Hmm, I don't know, want to pick a movie?"

"Sure," I replied, scrolling to the movie channels.

Shawshank Redemption, A Leap of Faith, Up, and *The Expendables* were all playing.

"Shawshank?" she asked, and I smiled.

"Perfect."

I started eating my kung pao chicken and realized I hadn't offered her a drink.

Feeling like an ass, I stood up and asked, "What can I fetch you to drink? I've got beer, water, and maybe some juice."

"Beer sounds good."

We finished our food and the movie, and I found myself sitting in my recliner awkward and nervous and unsure what to do next.

What the fuck is wrong with me? I wondered. I never had a problem being intimate with a woman. At least, *physically*, and I guess that answered my question. I was unsure of how to proceed because Dru had come to matter, and I was afraid I'd fuck it all up.

"Want another beer?" I asked.

"No, that's okay," Dru said, looking at me with a sly smile. "What I really want is for you to come over here."

She patted the cushion next to where she was sitting and added, "I promise I'll be gentle."

I made a sound somewhere between a cough and a chuckle.

Chiding myself for acting like a teenaged boy alone with a girl for the first time, I got up and went over to do as she requested.

As soon as I sat down, Dru moved into my arms and snuggled in, hugging me to her and resting her cheek on my chest. It felt nice. Great actually. I wasn't sure why she needed a blanket, because she was warm and soft against me.

In fact, if I had her in my bed, I wouldn't need a blanket, she'd be cozy enough.

The mental image of Dru in my bed was enough to bring home the fact that she was in my arms right now. I felt her breasts against me, the softness of her skin brushing against mine, and the smell of her hair, which held hints of cinnamon and spice.

No longer unsure of how I wanted to proceed, I eased Dru's head off my chest and brushed her lips with mine. Slowly at first . . . testing, and when she parted her lips, I deepened the kiss.

She made little sounds, like soft moans of happiness as we got lost in each other.

Dru laid back on the couch and I followed, never breaking

contact as I fit my body over hers, careful not to crush her with my weight. Her hands began to explore, traveling over my shoulders to my back, then under my shirt.

The first touch of her fingers on my skin had a groan escaping from my lips and I instinctively thrust against her, moaning louder when my cock moved against her heated pussy. *Fuck*, I could tell we were going to fit perfectly, and the sudden need to rid us of every stitch was immediate.

Dru bucked up against me, making the torture even sweeter.

Tearing my lips from hers, I began an exploration of my own, kissing my way across her jaw and down her silky soft neck. I stayed there for a few moments, nuzzling and tonguing the sensitive area, loving the way she moved beneath me, and the sounds she made.

Knowing if I didn't stop this soon, I was going to either take her on the couch, or end up with an epic case of blue balls, I pushed up off of her and struggled to catch my breath.

"We should stop," I managed, my hand still caressing her thigh as if of its own volition.

Dru shook her head.

"I don't want to stop. Do you? Really?"

"*Fuck, no,*" I admitted.

She beamed at my response.

"We're adults. Friends. And, I hope this means we'll be something more. Now, if you're not feeling the same way, then yes, I agree, we should stop, because I don't want to end up hurt . . . *but*, if you *do* feel the same way, and you want to see where this thing between us is going, then I think we should go to bed."

I stood up, loving how candid she was . . . *how fucking fearless* . . . and held out my hand.

"Let's go to bed," I replied.

She answered by putting her hand in mine.

Twenty-Five

Dru

He guided me down the hall to the door at the end that led to his bedroom.

All I kept thinking was, *this is happening, this is happening, this is happening . . .*

I was giddy, turned on, and full of anticipation. It was a Molotov cocktail of emotions, and I loved it.

My eyes flitted from his wide, muscular back, down to his tight ass, and back up again, and I could not wait to put my hands all over him. It felt like I'd been on simmer all day, ever since I watched him spar, and now I was ready to boil.

The master bedroom was large, with a huge king-sized bed, no headboard or footboard, just four large pillows at the top of a plain blue comforter. He had a dresser, another recliner in the corner, and a TV mounted on the wall. I could see two doors, which I assumed were for the master bath and his closet.

"Can I pop into the restroom really quick?" I asked.

"It's that one," Mick replied, pointing to the door on the left and letting my hand go.

"Thanks. Be right back."

His bathroom was nicely done, and I wondered briefly if he'd done it himself, like the kitchen.

I used the restroom, washed my hands, and checked myself out in the mirror.

Not terrible, but we can do better, I thought, then quickly shucked my jeans and blouse.

I was wearing a matching pink lace bra and panty set, so that was good. I gently opened a door, trying to be quiet. I didn't want to snoop, I just wanted the toothpaste I was sure was inside. When I found it, I put a little on my finger and used it to brush my teeth, or at the very least, freshen my mouth.

Chinese food and beer might taste great going down, but wasn't as much of a treat when you're making out.

After I rinsed my mouth, I tried my best to wipe the smudges from my mascara from under my eyes, finger brushed my hair, and fluffed it out. I turned to walk back out, then had a thought, quickly smelled my armpits, and turned back to the sink. I grabbed a washcloth, put some soap and water on it, and rubbed it under my arms really quick, then tossed the washcloth in the hamper.

Feeling better, but a little anxious about presenting myself in my underwear, I opened the door and struck my best sexy pose.

Mick's head swung toward me at the sound of the door opening, his eyes heating as they perused my near-naked form. He'd turned the bed down, which struck me as sweet, and was standing at the edge of it wearing a pair of gym shorts and nothing else.

"Looks like we had the same idea," I said, my voice throaty at the sight of him.

Mick turned so he was facing me, then crooked his finger in a *come here* gesture.

Needing to touch him again, to *feel* him, I hurried over to him as fast as my bare feet would allow, stopping just before I slammed my body into his. My hands went right to his chest, where they wanted to be, and I ran them over the smooth muscles, feeling a quiver run through me as I did.

"You look beautiful," he said, gruffly, his hand palming my cheek.

"So, do you," I breathed, remembering the first time he'd said that to me, at Tasha and Jericho's wedding party.

He grinned and lowered his head toward mine.

I closed my eyes, waiting with delicious anticipation for his lips to touch mine. And when they did, it was like something had ignited between us. There was no plotting or thought, only movement and feeling.

I moved in so I could feel the heat of his body flush against mine. His hard length brushed against my core, feeling so amazing that I couldn't stop myself from thrusting forward, eager for more.

Mick kissed the base of my throat, then moved lower, running his lips over the mounds of my breasts above my bra, nibbling the flesh lightly. Wanting more of that, I reached behind me to undo the clasp, then let it fall forward, shifting until it was completely off.

A low growl escaped Micks lips, then his arms came around my back as his mouth kissed my aching nipple.

I got a little dizzy from the pleasure and placed one hand at the back of his head, not only to steady myself, but to urge him to keep on doing what he was doing. He bit the tip softly, causing me to gasp, then moved on to love my other breast.

Wanting to participate, and bring him the kind of knee-buckling pleasure he was giving me, I reached in between us and placed my hand on his abs.

God everything about him feels so good . . .

I enjoyed the feel of his taut stomach briefly, then moved down, eager to feel the length of him. Dipping my hands beneath his shorts, I was pleased to find his hard cock waiting with no further barrier. So, I reached in and wrapped my hand around him, moving it up and down. Slowly at first, then faster.

"Fuck, Dru, you feel so good," Mick managed, as he dropped kisses along my chest.

Swiftly, he moved, lifting me up so I lost hold of him, and grasping on to my ass. My hands flew to his shoulders to hold steady as he spun me around and laid me on the edge of the bed in one swift movement.

Before I could sit up or make a move, his mouth was on me, kissing through the lace of my panties.

I had a brief moment of worry, where I thought, *I should have taken that wash cloth down south*, but then I couldn't care less.

Mick moved my panties to the side and nuzzled his nose in my pussy before licking me thoroughly and growling into me. *Holy shit*, he felt good. So good that I wasn't sure if I should buck into his face and come right then, or move away to try and draw it out.

I fisted my hand in his hair and looked down my torso at him. He was watching me with those sexy-as-hell eyes. I almost came on the spot.

"*Wait,* I'm gonna . . ." I paused, bowing my back and flinging my head to the side as the orgasm slammed through me.

Mick kept at my clit until I could take it no more, then slid up my body and kissed the side of my neck softly.

"I didn't want to come so fast," I panted, not really regretful at all.

I felt his chuckle against my neck.

"We'll just have to get you there again."

I caught my breath and turned into him, my hands caressing

his chest and paying special attention to his nipples, before making their descent.

I kissed his pec as I found his cock once more, this time fisting it tightly and jacking.

I was nipping at his nipple when Mick urged, *"Ride me."*

Surprised and pleased to be given control right out of the gate, I shifted up to sitting and let him get situated on the bed, before removing my panties and placing my hands on the waistband of his shorts.

As I eased his gym shorts down and tossed them on the floor, Mick reached in his drawer, grabbed a condom, and handed it to me.

I threw my leg over to straddle him, then folded over to kiss him. A brush against the lips quickly turned to madness. His hands in my hair, our tongues mashing, bodies writhing, the feel of skin on skin bringing us to the brink.

So, by the time I broke the kiss, I was more than ready to *ride him* and bring us both the satisfaction we were craving.

I opened the condom and rolled it on, grinning as Mick's eyes shuttered at the sensation of me handling him, then scooted up until I was over him. I placed my hands on his chest, then lowered myself slowly until I felt the tip of him at my entrance.

Yes.

I eased down slowly, then back up, teasing us this way repeatedly until Mick could take it no longer and thrust up, filling me with him. I gasped at the feeling of being fully seated on him. Mick's hands came to my hips and his eyes looked glazed as I started to move.

I rocked slowly at first, pausing every few beats to raise slightly off him and slam back down, then, when it looked like Mick's eyes were about to roll back in his head, and I felt the pressure within me begin to build, I quickened the pace.

Mick helped me along, moving my hips rapidly as my movements began to get shakier as I rode my way to our release.

"*Fuck, yes, Dru, faster,*" Mick growled, but I was already gone, clenching around him as my vision began to blur and I saw stars.

I squeezed around him one more time, and watched with dazed eyes as his face filled with ecstasy. His hands kept my hips moving as he rode out his orgasm, then I collapsed against his chest.

"Holy crap," I panted. "That was even better than I'd imagined. And I did *a lot* of imagining."

I felt Mick's laugh against my cheek.

"Next time, I get to take your clothes off myself."

I murmured my agreement and began to drift off.

Twenty-Six

Mick

*T*urned out, I *didn't* get to take her clothes off the next time, because it happened in the middle of the night and we were still both naked.

You didn't hear me complaining, though.

There's nothing better than waking up with a naked woman in your bed, feeling her hands on your body, and being able to slide inside and feel her squeeze you like a glove. It was hot as hell, and the only way I wanted to wake up for the rest of my life.

I'd always known there was an attraction, and chemistry, even though I did my best to ignore it, but what transpired in my bed was unlike anything I'd ever experienced.

You know how people always say, *when you meet the one, you'll know it*, and all us bachelors would scoff and blow them off? Well, I was beginning to think that shit was legit. After spending the last few months getting to know Dru, and moving relatively slow as far as relationships go, and then experiencing not only the connection between us in bed, but the way I feel just being with her? I knew the things I felt for her were feelings I'd never had for anyone before.

It was kind of freaking me out, but, oddly enough, not in a bad way.

My ma was gonna have a field day.

I still had the sweet taste of Dru on my lips after giving her head again this morning and thought I just may have found my happy place.

Now, I was making pancakes and bacon as Dru took a shower since we both had to get back to our regular work schedule today. I'd promised to shadow her at work on Friday and we were meeting at her place for dinner tonight, so at least I had that to look forward to.

"Smells good," Dru said, walking up behind me in yesterday's clothes, her hair wrapped up in a wet bun.

"So do you," I said as she put her arms around me.

"I hope you don't mind, I borrowed a pair of your underwear."

I turned to look at her and grinned.

"You did?"

"I couldn't wear the same pair I wore yesterday," she said, wrinkling up her nose. "I have to go home and change first anyway, but yours worked in a pinch."

She looks fucking adorable . . . Shit, I was starting to sound like Jackson.

"They'd have to be practically falling off of you, even if they are boxer briefs," I said, looking down between us and wondering what they looked like on her.

"Yeah, the jeans are pretty much holding them up."

I kissed her briefly on the lips and said, "Let's get this food in you so you can get on your way to work. I don't want to get in trouble for making you late."

Dru shrugged.

"I doubt Millie's even coming in today, and I don't have anything pressing this morning. It'll be fine. But, I am hungry, so . . ."

She took the plate from me and took it to the dining room.

As I watched her walk away, I thought, *this is worth a break in my routine any day of the week.*

We ate breakfast and I dropped her off before heading to the office to begin my day.

It went by pretty quickly, and I was happy to get a text from Jackson, saying he wanted to get together at the bar the next night with the guys to have a drink and see what's been going on. It had been a few weeks since we'd been able to get together, outside of all the wedding stuff, just us guys.

I was looking forward to it.

What I didn't know, and probably needed to find out, was whether I was supposed to say anything to the guys about me and Dru.

Were we a couple? Exclusive? Out in public?

Why the hell am I thinking about this shit? And, where'd my balls go?

Still, I didn't want to say anything if she wasn't ready. I was in uncharted territory here.

Just as I was shutting down for the night, an email popped up in my inbox. I checked the time, then opened it up when I saw I had time.

It was from Susan Temple.

Mr. O'Donnelly,

Good evening. I got your information from my receptionist, Dani. She said that you're a private investigator and that you were looking into my husband. I'm afraid she was under the assumption I'd hired you, and I let her believe so in order to find out what she knew.

I would like to hire you in order to get proof of my husband's infidelity. I believe you may already have what I need at your fingertips, and I'd like to have whatever ammunition I can when I file for divorce.

I look forward to hearing from you.

vr,

Susan Temple

I stared at my computer screen, rereading the email a couple times, before shutting down without replying.

I was going to have to think about this one, and talk to Dru before I took the case.

Yes, it was true that I already had photographs and documentation in my possession, which would prove that *good ole Johnson* was having yet another affair, but I didn't know how Dru would feel about me taking on the woman who'd stolen her father away for a client.

It felt good to think of someone else's feelings before coming to a decision, even if it was a business one, and I found I really liked the fact that I had Dru to "go home" to after work and discuss the events of my day, while she told me hers.

Maybe I'd been wrong about relationships.

This one seemed to suit me just fine.

Twenty-Seven

Dru

*A*ll day I'd felt like I was floating on a cloud.

I was pretty sure I'd annoyed most of the staff, but I didn't care. I was *happy*.

It felt like after a year of watching Millie and Tasha fall in love, it was finally my turn. And, getting to know Mick first as a friend and professional, before becoming lovers, made the fall all the sweeter.

Lovers.

I loved that word.

Even more, I loved the fact that that's exactly what we were. *Lovers.*

That's just the kind of talk that's been making everyone sick all day, Dru, I chided myself, but my insides were so mushy I didn't care.

Let them think I was a sappy, lovesick woman.

I was happy to be.

I wrapped up my work early, with a smile on my face, and wished everyone a good night, before walking to the market to pick up items to make dinner.

Mick was coming over and I was going to cook for him for the first time. It seemed like a big deal. *A moment.* And one I didn't want to screw up. His pancakes that morning had been perfection, or maybe that had been the afterglow.

Who knew.

All I knew was that I needed to find the best steak, the biggest potatoes, and the plumpest asparagus the grocery store had, because I wanted to make my big hulk of a man a meal he could really sink his teeth into.

I walked the aisles, throwing items in my basket as I whistled my way through the store.

When I was standing in the checkout line, my phone pinged with a notification and I opened it to see I had a message on Instagram.

Hey Drew, it's Brody. I wanted to let you know that I went to see my brothers and told them about you guys. They were surprised, but excited, and we'd like to plan a trip out there to meet you all. Is that okay?

My stomach did a little somersault of joy as I read Brody's words.

Of course, I wanted to meet them, but I needed to tell Millie and Tasha about everything I'd learned first.

Hi, Brody, I'm so happy to hear from you! Tasha is still on her honeymoon, but we'd love for you all to come visit. Let me talk to my sisters when she's back and I'll let you know a good weekend to come down. Talk to you soon, Dru.

I'd checked out and made it halfway back to my place when my phone chimed again.

SMH, so sorry about sp your name wrong. I'll let my brothers know and talk to you later. B

I walked the rest of the way home with a smile, thinking this day couldn't get any better, when I saw Mick getting out of his Jeep.

Looks like I was wrong, it just got better . . .

"Hey, beautiful, what put that smile on your face?" he asked as he strode toward me.

My cheeks felt tired with all the smiling I'd been doing today, but I managed to smile even wider at his greeting.

"Other than seeing you again?" I asked coyly, not even feeling embarrassed by how cheesy that sounded. I loved the cheese. "I got a message from Brody, my brother; he said they're interested in coming down to meet us."

"That's great, I knew they'd want to get to know you. Here, let me take those," Mick said, taking the bags I was carrying.

"Thanks."

"Did you have a good day?" he asked as we went up the stairs.

"Yes, very productive. You?"

"Yeah, mine was productive, too. There's something I wanted to talk to you about, actually."

I let us in and went to the kitchen to start getting out everything I needed, while Mick set the bags on the counter.

"Okay, you can talk while I cook," I replied, taking out Millie's recipe for the perfect steak.

I started two pots of water to boil in, turned the oven up high to roast the asparagus, and seasoned the meat to let it rest for a few minutes before cooking.

"An email came in right as I was leaving the office," he began, crossing to the fridge and pulling out a beer. "Want one?" he asked.

"No thanks, I think I'll have wine instead."

Mick put his beer on the counter and grabbed the bottle of red I had in my wine rack.

He continued as he opened the bottle. "It was from Susan Temple. She wants to hire me to get evidence that your dad is cheating. Sounds like she's gonna divorce him."

"Wow," I said, trying to figure out how I felt about that, then decided I didn't care. He deserved no less. "What did you say?"

"Nothing yet, I wanted to talk it over with you first. Get your feelings on it."

I finished putting the potatoes in one of the pots and turned to him.

"Really? But, it's your job. I don't want to interfere with your work," I said honestly, then added, "But I appreciate you thinking of me."

"I don't want to take on a case that's going to make you uncomfortable," Mick said, pulling me into his arms.

I held on tight and listened to the sound of his hear beating.

"That's very sweet," I murmured against his chest.

"I know we haven't talked about us, or defined anything yet, but on my end? I'm all in. I'm into you, and I want to see where this goes. I don't want to see other people, and I want us to tell everyone we know that we're together. And, *being together* means that I want your input on things, and I don't want to do anything that's going to hurt you, or put you in a bad position. I have your back, and I hope you'll have mine."

My heart swelled in my chest and my eyes welled at his proclamation.

I leaned back and looked up into his handsome face, which had become so precious to me.

"That all sounds fantastic, and I agree one-hundred percent," I replied with a happy, goofy smile. "We'll plan a dinner next week when Tasha and Jericho are back, and tell everyone. And, as far as Susan goes, I think you should take the case."

"Are you sure?"

"Absolutely," I replied. "Now, let me go so I don't burn your dinner. Can you get the ice out for me? I'm going to blanch the asparagus before I roast them."

"Yup," he said, then a few seconds later asked, "Uh, is there something you want to tell me?"

"What?" I asked, turning my head to look at him.

He had the freezer door opened wide so I could see the inside shelves on the door, which were loaded with Ben & Jerry's ice cream.

"Oh," I said with a giggle. "You found me out . . . I love ice cream."

"There are like, ten different flavors in here. Who can eat that much ice cream?"

"Uh, wait, you're not saying you don't like ice cream, are you? Cause, that could be a deal breaker," I joked.

"I like ice cream as much as any *regular* person does," Mick said, his voice full of laughter. "But this seems like a bit much."

"First off, look how small those containers are, they don't last long. Second, I never know what flavor I'm going to be in the mood for. *The Tonight Dough, Chunky Monkey, Peanut Butter Cup, Phish Food, Half-Baked* . . . I mean, what if I had a bad day and only *Salted Caramel Almond* will do?"

Mick was looking at me like I was cracked, so I asked, "Have you ever *tried* Ben & Jerry's?"

"No, but I've had *ice cream*."

"It's not the same thing, you'll see," I promised. "We'll pop your *Cherry Garcia* tonight."

Twenty-Eight

Mick

"Can I get a round of shots and another pitcher of beer?" I asked the bartender the next night.

We were meeting up for our dude's night out and everyone was there except Jackson, who was on his way.

I went back to our usual table with the pitcher, while the bartender followed with a tray of shots.

Ty, Rob, Hector, and I had been there for about fifteen minutes and had already finished off one pitcher of beer. Seemed like we'd all needed this hang out. It had been way too long. Hector was our newest edition. As Jericho's best friend, he'd started joining us when Tasha and Jericho had gotten back together.

I didn't know him well, but he seemed like a good guy.

"Anyone catch the game last night? Man, the Cowboys got spanked," Ty asked after thanking the bartender for his shot.

"Yeah, that shit was brutal. Glad none of those guys are on my fantasy team," Rob replied.

"Well, aren't you all a sight for sore eyes."

We all looked up to see Jackson walking toward us looking

happy as hell.

"Nice tan," Ty said.

As Rob called out, "Boy, I can tell you've had a break from the classroom. You look relaxed."

I stood up and clasped his hand with one of my own and clapped his shoulder with the other.

"Lookin' good, Heeler."

"How was the honeymoon?" Hector asked.

"Thanks," Jackson said to me, squeezing my hand tight before letting it go. "The honeymoon was great. If you can lounge on a beach with a beautiful woman and have absolutely no responsibilities for seven days, I highly recommend it. That kind of thing shouldn't be reserved for honeymoons alone, I think it should be an annual occurrence."

"Can we get this man a shot?" I asked, and Ty grabbed the spare shot and handed it to him.

We all raised our shot glasses.

"To Heeler and Millie, the honeymoon's over," Rob said, and we all started laughing.

"Nice," Jackson said wryly, and we all did the shot.

We all settled back into our seats around the table and Hector poured Jackson a beer.

"So, what did I miss?" Jackson asked cheerfully.

He looked to Rob.

"Jan's letting me eat red meat once a week . . . I call that a win."

We all chuckled and Jackson turned to Hector.

"Been busy at the restaurant with Jericho gone, but I did squeeze in a date with Tanisha."

"Millie's Tanisha? From Three Sisters?" Jackson asked.

"The one and only," Hector said with a grin, and I could see he really liked her.

"Wow, cool," Jackson said, then turned to Ty.

"Well, I was gonna wait until the end-of-year talent show, but couldn't . . . So, I asked Rebecca to marry me at the annual carnival."

"What? That's fantastic!" Jackson exclaimed, getting up and rounding the table to give his buddy a quick hug.

By the grin on Rob's face, I guessed he'd already known. Since Ty, Rebecca, Rob, and Jackson all worked at the high school, it was no surprise. They were all thick as thieves.

"Where did you do it?" I asked, genuinely happy for the guy.

"Got down on one knee in front of the kissing booth. The kids went wild," Ty replied with a huge grin.

"I bet," Jackson said as he sat back down. "Wow, that's crazy. What about you, Mick, any news to share?"

I thought about Dru wanting to wait to tell her sisters, but knew I couldn't keep it from these guys any longer, not after they were sharing the stuff in their lives. Plus, I was excited and proud to call Dru mine.

"Actually, we wanted to wait to tell everyone until Tasha and Jericho are back, but I think you guys can keep a secret," I began.

"This sounds good," Rob said, leaning forward on the table.

"It is," I agreed. "*Very* good."

"Well, don't keep us in suspense, Mick, what is it?"

"Dru and I are together."

Jackson sat back, his face full of shock.

"Seriously?" he asked.

"That's great man, Dru's the best," Ty said, and I nodded at him, but my eyes were trained on Jackson.

"What, you don't think it's a good idea?" I asked, not sure what I was feeling, but not liking it.

"Huh? No, that's not it at all. I think it's *the best* idea, I'm just surprised, that's all. I mean, Millie mentioned wanting to hook the two of you up, but said that you weren't into it. Not that she wasn't still going to try . . . She's planning to have you guys over for dinner next week, once Jericho and Tasha were back. It's her big matchmaking scheme. Guess it's moot now."

"Nah, like I said, Dru wants to wait and tell her sisters together, so let Millie set it up and that's when we can make our big reveal," I suggested.

"That works," Jackson said. "Boy, will she be surprised."

"You guys cool with keeping it under wraps until then?" I asked the guys.

They all agreed and we started talking about football.

"Hey," Hector said, leaning in to me. "I'm happy for you and Dru. I know she's been into you for a while now. It's great news."

"Thanks, man," I replied with a grin, then went back to talking sports with my friends.

Twenty-Nine

Dru

"Wake up, sleepy head, time to start the day," I whispered. I was leaning over Mick, who was fast asleep in my bed, looking adorable and rumpled.

It was his turn to follow my *day in the life*, so he'd stayed the night last night. Not that we'd gotten much sleep, which is why he was still dead to the world, his large frame taking up over half of my bed.

I was too excited to sleep, and had gotten up early to shower and make him breakfast.

I put my hand on his shoulder and ran it lovingly down his arm.

"Mick," I tried again, then squealed when his arm shot out and he pulled me onto the bed.

He rolled me under him smoothly, shoved his face into my neck, and nuzzled me.

"Morning," he said gruffly.

"Good morning," I said with a giggle, wiggling beneath him. "Breakfast is ready."

"Mmmmm," he murmured against my neck as he kissed me, his lips soft and warm. "What's for breakfast?"

"Eggs, bacon, hash browns, and toast."

"Sounds delish," Mick said, then nipped my neck lightly.

"Come on, we have to eat and get down to work," I said, before reaching up to cradle his face in my palm.

He gave me a smile and kiss on the lips, then rolled off of me and held out his hand to help me up.

We ate breakfast, then I cleaned up while he showered and got ready for the day.

I was a little unsure of what I was going to say to Millie when she inevitably asked why he was shadowing me, but figured I'd cross that bridge when I came to it. I knew Mick had already told the guys about us, but I was pretty sure Jackson had kept his promise and not told Millie. Otherwise I would have heard about it by now.

We went downstairs and into Three Sisters, the smell of fresh baked bread hitting us as soon as we opened the door.

"Oh, man," Mick said, practically drooling. "Do you get to taste test, or . . ."

I laughed.

"If Millie's trying out a new recipe we do, but day to day that's left up to the kitchen staff. Millie does usually keep food in separate containers for us for lunch, so we're lucky that way."

"Not a bad gig," Mick said with a grin, sniffing the air and patting his stomach.

"There's no way you can be hungry after what you just ate," I replied with a laugh. "Come on, I'll show you the office and then we can go out and I'll introduce you around. Oh, and if you want to take some of Millie's food with you to your mom's for lunch, feel free. We have plenty."

"I figured since I was shadowing you, I'd be with you for lunch. I told Ma not to expect me. She was actually happy about it, when

I told her the reason."

I stopped walking and put my hand on his arm.

"Mick, no, I don't want you to do that. Visiting with your mom is an important part of your day; when I came up with this idea I didn't mean to take that away. In fact, I'd go with you, but I have a lunch meeting with a client, so I can't. You should definitely go, though."

Mick looked down at me, his eyes full of something I couldn't pinpoint.

"You're amazing," he said, putting his hand behind my head as he leaned down to kiss me soundly.

When he pulled back, I grinned up at him. "You're pretty hot shit yourself."

Mick chuckled and followed me back to the office.

"Don't mind my clutter, it may look messy, but I swear, I know where everything is," I said when we stepped inside. "You can hang out at Tasha's much more organized desk today. That one's Millie's, she spends most of her time in the kitchen though, and doesn't use it much."

He looked around and said, "I'd say this office is a pretty good testament to who you all are as people."

"How so?" I asked, trying to see it through his eyes.

"Well, Tasha's desk is neat as a pin, organized so much that even her paper clips are separated by color. She has a *What to Expect When You're Expecting* book on her shelf, tabbed out and color coded, and she already has a picture of her and Jericho on her desk from their wedding celebration. She must have gone right out and got it printed and framed."

I nodded. That was Natasha to a T. Not only organized, but quick to get things accomplished and almost anal in her need to have tasks completed.

"Now, Millie's is against the wall, not out in the open like yours and Tasha's. She's more low-key, likes to be in the background, rather than the star of the show. Her shelf is half cookbooks and half Elvis biographies. She has a corkboard with Kayla's artwork and recipe cards tacked to it, along with a poem by Keats, which probably makes her think of Jackson every time she lays eyes on it."

"Wow, you're really good at this," I whispered, thinking he knew my sisters well.

"Well, it comes with the territory," he replied.

"And, me?" I asked.

Mick opened his mouth to reply, then closed it when Millie walked in.

"Mick!" she exclaimed when she saw him. "What are you doing here? I've actually been hoping to run in to you."

Millie looked between Mick and me, a gleam in her eye, and waited for his response.

He crossed to give her a kiss on the cheek.

"Morning, Millie, you look beautiful . . . happy."

Millie and I were fraternal twins, but looked so similar that people often thought we were identical. I never quite understood how. Millie had a sweetness about her that just brightened any room she walked in to.

Today she was wearing her black chef coat, with her hair pulled back in a bun and her face devoid of makeup.

She still looked stunning.

"I am," Millie replied, her face beaming. "The vacation was just what we needed, but we were so happy to get back home."

"I bet. To answer your questions, I'm shadowing Dru for a bit to-day. It's kind of like, research . . . to help out with one of my cases."

Nice save, I thought. Although I hated fibbing to my sister, I really didn't think she'd mind. She'd be so happy once she found out Mick and I were together.

"Oh, nice. I was hoping we could finally have you over for that dinner we talked about before, once Tasha and Jericho are back. Just the six of us," Millie said, her eyes shifting to include me in the conversation.

"Sure, that sounds good," Mick replied.

"Perfect," Millie said, obviously pleased that he'd agreed so easily. "Does Monday night work for you? That's our day off."

He nodded, not letting on that he already knew what my day off was, and Millie clapped her hands together.

"Oh, I'm so excited. Are there any foods you don't eat, or are allergic to?" she asked, ever the professional chef.

"Nope, I'm an equal opportunity eater," Mick replied, and my sister and I laughed.

He's going to fit into this family just fine.

Thirty

Mick

It was finally here.

The night of Millie's dinner party, where Dru and I would finally come clean with everyone, except Jackson, of course, who already knew. Still, I didn't like keeping it from Millie when I saw her, or feeling like we had something to hide.

I was ready to lay it all out on the table.

And, I was pumped to see Jericho and ask how their trip to Bali went.

I'd always liked Jackson's house. It had a big, open floor plan, and welcoming feel. It was even cozier now that Millie had moved in and put her touches on the space.

"Hi, Mick, oh . . . Dru, you're here, too, yay!" Millie said from the kitchen as Jackson let Dru and me inside.

"Hey, Mills, need help?" Dru asked, making a beeline for her twin.

"How's it going, brother?" I asked Jackson as I walked inside.

"Pretty good. Getting ready for standardized testing at school, but I've got a pretty good group of kids this year. How about you?

Any new exciting cases?" he asked.

"A few. You guys will actually hear about one of them later, but I'll let Dru take lead on that," I replied.

Jackson looked at me for a moment, then said, "Okay . . . more secrets, huh?"

"Not after tonight," I said, the relief evident in my tone.

"Good, well, until then, how about a drink?"

"You got whiskey?" I asked.

"That serious?"

"It's gonna cause a bit of a stir, but I think these sisters are made of stern stuff."

Worry crossed Jackson's face.

"Now you're starting to freak me out."

I clapped him on the back and said, "We'll get through it. Let's get that drink."

Jackson was pouring us each a glass when the front door opened again and the grinning duo of Natasha and Jericho came rushing in.

"*We're back!*" Natasha cried, heading straight for her sisters.

The women squealed and hugged each other while jumping up and down. I wasn't sure how they managed it, but they did.

Jericho came over to shake our hands, and Jackson offered him a drink.

"How was Bali?" he asked.

"It was amazing, actually," Jericho replied. "More interesting, fun, and adventurous than I'd imagined when I booked it. We had the perfect time."

"That's awesome, Smythe, you both deserved it, after the craziness you've been through," I said.

"Ain't that the truth," he replied with a wry grin, his eyes catching on his wife. "She was a little sick at the beginning of the trip, but luckily, it passed."

"You ready to be a father?" Jackson asked, smiling at his own daughter Kayla, who'd just joined the ladies in the kitchen.

"You know, I really am. I used to think I didn't want to be a dad, mostly cause mine was a piece of shit, but now, the reality of having a baby with Tash makes me the happiest man alive."

Jackson nodded in agreement, and I immediately searched out Dru, wondering what it would be like if we started a family together. Would I be excited like Jericho, or scared shitless? As I watched her laughing with her sisters, I realized I'd be competing with Smythe for that happiest man alive title.

Huh. Wasn't that a kick in the pants.

Dinner was a loud and jolly affair, with Millie's amazing cooking and both couple's tales of their adventures while on their honeymoons.

After Kayla had gone to get ready for bed, and we were sitting in the living room, having drinks and continuing conversation, Dru looked at me and nodded, and I knew it was time for us to come clean. About everything.

Dru looked nervous, but my girl took a deep breath and put her fearless face on.

"Okay, so, I've been waiting for you both to get home to tell you some big news. Actually, it's like a three-parter of big news."

Millie put her glass down and put her hand on Dru's knee, as if sensing her anxiety, while Tasha leaned forward in her chair and gave Dru her full attention.

"First off, I'll start with the easy one. Mick and I are dating," she said, shooting a smile at me.

"What? That's great!" Millie exclaimed, looking at us happily.

"It really is," Natasha agreed.

"Congrats, man," Jericho said, clapping me on the shoulder.

When Jackson didn't say anything, Millie looked at him with narrowed eyes.

"Did you know?" she accused.

Jackson shrugged sheepishly.

"Mick told us at the bar, but I was sworn to secrecy."

"But, we're married now, Jackson. Married people don't have to uphold secrecy laws, they tell each other everything."

"Even when it concerns your sister and she wanted to tell you herself?" He asked.

Millie sighed and said, "Fine, I'll give you a pass. *This time.* But no more secrets, got it?"

"Yes, ma'am," Jackson said with a grin and a little two-finger salute.

"Smartass," she mumbled, then looked back at Dru. "Okay, forget that, tell us everything. When did it happen?"

"Well," Dru began, looking at me for support. I nodded and put my arm around her back. "I liked him right away, but he wouldn't date me at first, because he doesn't date clients."

"Clients?" Natasha asked, not missing a thing. "Did you hire Mick?"

"Yes, I did. To find our father. And, he found him."

There was a stunned silence.

I looked at Millie, who looked on the brink of tears, and Natasha, who looked furious, and thought, *oh shit.*

"You did what?" Natasha asked, her voice full of anger.

"Tash," Jericho said gently, trying to reach out for her, but she scooted away and looked at Dru accusingly.

"We agreed never to look for him. Why would you do that? Lie to us? Go behind or backs?"

"It wasn't like that," Dru explained. "I needed to find him, to get closure and to tell him about Mom. I wanted to see his face and ask him why he left, why he never came back."

"But, you promised," Millie said, her voice filled with pain.

"I know I did, but it wasn't about you, either of you, it was about me. And, actually, I never would have even told you guys that I found him, if I hadn't found out something that you both need to know."

"I don't need to know anything about that man," Tasha spit out, obviously furious.

"You'll want to know this," Dru insisted. "We have brothers. Three of them."

Millie gasped and covered her mouth as tears slid down her face.

"I don't care. They aren't my brothers, not if they're from *him*."

"Natasha," Dru chided. "You don't mean that."

"I do mean that, and honestly, I'm so mad at you right now I can't even look at you. I can't believe you went behind our backs like this, after the pact we made." Natasha stood up and looked at Jericho. "We need to go."

Dru's face fell and she looked to her twin.

"Mills?"

Millie shook her head and said, "You shouldn't have."

Dru stood up and hurried out of the room, down the hall toward the bathroom.

"Let's go," Natasha said, while her sister curled into Jackson's arms.

"Wait," I said, standing and using a firm tone. "You both need to understand that this wasn't about you, or about the pact you made as sisters. This was about Dru and her need to follow through with something that was weighing on her. You both dealt with your father's leaving in your own way, well . . . Dru wasn't dealing with it, and she hired me because she needed to face the man who she felt was holding her back. She needed to look him in the eyes and tell him what was on her heart. For *herself*. If you don't want to see your father again, that's your choice; in fact, I'd highly recommend you leave that asshole in your rearview, but this was something she needed to do. She doesn't need your permission, or anger, she only needs your support. She's always the first one to back both of you, and now it's your turn to have her back. I get that you're angry, that you may need to sleep on it and come to terms with your own feelings on the subject, but I'll not have you making Dru feel bad for doing what she needs to for her own peace of mind. Now, I'm going to take Dru and go home, but I expect you to talk to her tomorrow and apologize for making her feel like shit."

I started to walk toward the hall the way Dru had gone, but stopped and turned to say, "And Dru's very excited about meeting your brothers. Again, it's your choice if you want to have anything to do with them or not, but they *will* be coming here, and she *will* be letting them into her life."

With that final shot, I went in search of Dru. As soon as I turned the corner, she flew into my arms.

"Thank you," she said, her hands holding my head still as she rained kisses all over my face. "No one has ever stuck up for me like that before."

"Get used to it," I answered, dropping a soft kiss on her lips before saying, "Let's get out of here."

Thirty-One

Dru

I walked in to work the next day feeling like a zombie.

I hadn't gotten much sleep. Too many thoughts and emotions kept me up while Mick slept soundly beside me.

My sisters and I had fought over the years, of course we had, but not as adults. At least, nothing like what had gone down at Millie's. Ours had always been skirmishes over clothes, boys, or soccer. Never something that had threatened to tear us apart like that.

Guilt invaded me, pushing between the pain and sadness, and I worried I'd done the wrong thing by hiring Mick in the first place.

Maybe I should have left well enough alone.

Even as the thought entered my head, I shook it out, remembering the amazing things Mick had said to my family in my defense last night. Seriously, it had almost been worth Millie's tears and Tasha's rage to hear Mick have my back like that.

He'd been amazing.

I straightened my spine and took a deep breath before entering my office, just in case one of my sisters was in there, waiting to pounce.

But, when I walked inside, it was empty, so I let out the breath, crossed to my desk, and got to work.

I'd gone through all of my emails and responded where needed, when I felt someone watching me. I lifted my head to see Millie standing in the doorway, looking unsure of herself. I could feel her sorrow, and hated to make my twin feel even an ounce of sadness.

I knew that she and Dad had been closest out of all of us, and that my finding him, and her learning what a jerk he'd turned out to be, was going to be hardest on her.

"Hey, Mills," I said softly. Being unsure of myself around her was a foreign feeling, and I hated it.

She took a few steps inside.

"I need to apologize to you. I was surprised when you announced you'd found Dad, and even hearing about him brought up those feelings of abandonment. My reaction was swift and instinctual, and I never meant to hurt you. Actually, Jackson and I stayed up talking last night, and I think I'm going to go see a therapist about it. After my reaction to Kayla's disappearance when Jackson and I were dating, and then the way grief overcame me last night when you talked about Dad, I realized that I haven't dealt with his abandonment of us, and I can't fix it on my own."

"Oh, Mills," I said, standing and moving to pull her in for a hug.

She wrapped her arms around me and we held each other for a few moments.

"I think it'll be good for you," I whispered, hating that she was hurting. "And, I'm sorry that I brought out those feelings."

"It's not your fault," Millie said, pulling back to look in my face.

It was comforting to stare into the eyes of the person you'd shared a womb with. No one could comfort me the way Millie could, and I just hoped I could give her some now.

"Mick was right. You're entitled to get the closure you need to move forward and try and put what he did to us in the past. We all need to do so in our own ways, and I think therapy will be my way."

I nodded.

"I don't want to see him," she admitted, her voice shaky.

"You don't have to," I replied firmly. "Honestly, you're better off remembering him the way he was . . . the person he was to you, *before*."

"After what Mick said, I figured as much. But, Dru, I would like to meet these brothers of ours, when they come to town."

I grinned.

"I knew you would! I've only met Brody, the youngest, and I honestly don't know anything about the other two yet, only that Dad and Susan are their parents. But, Brody seemed like a very nice kid. Sweet and laid back, and I can't hold the sins of his parents against him . . . against any of them."

"I agree," Millie said, taking a step back and wiping a few stray tears off her cheeks.

Just then, Tasha walked in, her face a mask of indifference.

She walked passed us both without saying a word, marching to her desk with a purpose.

Millie gave me a sad smile and said, "Well, I better get to work."

I nodded and watched her walk out, before going back to my desk.

"Tasha . . ." I began, but she cut me off.

"I can't talk about it yet, Dru. I need time," she said.

I sighed, my stomach in knots, and opened up my planner to see what the rest of my week looked like.

My phone rang and I saw Mick's name flash across the screen.

"Hey," I answered with a smile, grateful for the interruption.

"Ma's in the hospital," he said, panicked. "Can you meet me at Saint Mary's?"

"Yes, of course, I'm on my way," I exclaimed, standing and looking for my purse.

He hung up and I grabbed my bag, my heart pounding as I glanced at my calendar again.

"Can you have Tanisha take my one o'clock and check with the florist about tomorrow night's event?" I asked Natasha as I hurried to the door.

"What's wrong?" she asked from right behind me.

"Mick's mom's at Saint Mary's. I don't know what happened, but he asked me to come."

"Oh my God, poor Mick," Tasha said, her hand covering her mouth. Mick and Tasha had an interesting relationship, ever since he saved her from Jericho's mom and brought her back home safely. I knew they had a bond, and no matter how mad she was at me, she'd want to be there for Mick. "I'll tell Millie and have Tanisha and Claire cover for us. We'll be right behind you."

"Thanks, Natasha," I said, my eyes filling with tears. "And, I'm sorry."

"Let's not worry about that now," Tasha said with a wave of her hand. "Go."

I nodded and took off, eager to get to Mick and Dottie.

Thirty-Two

Mick

I rushed into the hospital, my heart in my throat.

I'd just been leaving the gym when the admin from Ma's facility had called to tell me she'd been taken to Saint Mary's. She'd fallen at breakfast that morning and had been taken in by an ambulance.

I knew it could have been worse. Thank God she didn't have a heart attack or something, but the thought of my ma being in the hospital was enough to make me frantic.

"Dottie O'Donnelly!" I shouted when I entered the emergency room, my voice louder than I'd intended. "Sorry," I managed to say in a more acceptable tone. "My mother was brought in this morning, Dottie O'Donnelly."

"Yes, sir, someone will be right out to take you back."

I looked at the chairs in the waiting area, then moved past them and started pacing in the aisle.

A few minutes later, a nurse came out and called out, "Mr. O'Donnelly?"

"Yes," I replied, hurrying toward her.

"Your mother is stable. We've moved her to a room on the second floor. You can follow me."

I breathed a little easier, knowing that it was good news for her to be out of the emergency room and stable.

Still, when I walked in and saw my mother looking frail and scared in the hospital bed, I felt like a little boy, rather than a grown ass man.

"Ma," I called, trying to keep my voice from shaking.

She looked away from the small TV mounted on the wall in front of her and said, "I'm not dead, Mickie, get over here and give me a kiss."

"Jesus, Ma, you scared me," I said as walked over to her bedside and leaned down to kiss her wrinkled cheek.

"Don't you take the Lord's name," she chided, causing me to smile for the first time since I'd gotten that call. "This is a Catholic hospital, for crying out loud."

I chucked.

"Sorry, Ma. What happened?"

She sighed, looking put out by the whole thing.

"I was going back to get cream cheese for my bagel and didn't realize Robert was standing behind me with his new cane. He's been taking that stupid thing everywhere, even though he can walk just fine without it. Anyway, I tripped over the darn thing and put out my hands to stop by fall, broke my left wrist."

I looked to her side and saw a cast was around her left wrist and partially over her hand.

"That's it, I'm taking you home with me," I told her, my tone brokering no argument.

Of course, she argued.

"Oh no, you're not. A broken wrist is no big deal, plus, I'll need a little extra help from the staff at the facility."

"I can help you," I replied.

"No, you have work and need to focus on Dru," she said. "How're things going with you two?"

"Great . . . But, I'm serious, Ma, you should move out of that place and live with me."

"No, but thanks, Mickie. I'm happy where I am."

I let out a frustrated growl and wanted to pull my hair out.

"Knock, knock, can I come in?"

I turned to see Dru standing in the doorway, her appearance exactly what I needed.

I crossed to her and took her in my arms.

"Thanks for coming," I murmured into her hair.

"Of course," she replied, patting my back.

I dropped a kiss on her forehead before letting her go.

Just her presence made me feel calmer.

"How are you feeling, Dottie?" Dru asked, and I realized she was carrying a bouquet of flowers.

"Oh, pshhh, it's only a broken wrist. Mickie shouldn't have made such a fuss," Ma said, but I could see she was pleased Dru had come.

"These are for you, should I put them in water?"

"Oh, just bring them here for now, we can get water later."

Dru took the flowers over and handed them to Ma as she sat on the edge of the bed.

"Hello!"

I turned to see Millie and Tasha coming inside.

"I hope we aren't intruding, but we wanted to check in on Mrs. O'Donnelly," Millie said, carrying a vase of flowers.

"Oh," Ma said, trying to sit up and fluff out her hair for the new arrivals.

"Dottie, I'd like you to meet my sisters, Millie and Natasha."

"It's lovely to meet you both."

I felt a hand on my arm and looked down to see Natasha standing next to me.

"She's okay?" she asked, worriedly.

I nodded.

"It's a broken wrist, so it'll heal. Thank *God*."

Natasha hugged my side briefly, then went to shake my ma's hand.

"Jackson and Jericho are coming by as soon as they can get a break from work," Millie told me from her perch on the other side of Ma's bed.

"Oh, they don't have to, I'm not sure how long they'll be keeping her," I replied, feeling foolish for making more out of the situation than it was.

"They want to," Tasha assured me. "If you guys leave before either of them arrives, just shoot 'em a text and let them know."

I nodded, looking around the room and thinking how lucky I was to have these women in my life. It was crazy to think that over a year ago, I had no idea who they were, and now they were an integral part of my life.

Especially Dru.

Thirty-Three

Dru

"I'm sorry I got so mad," Tasha said. "You know how Dad's a trigger for all of us. I was upset that you broke the pact, but we made that pact when we were kids. Mick was right, you deserve to do what you need to without getting grief from us. And, Dru . . . I'm ecstatic about you and Mick. I truly think you guys deserve each other."

"Thanks, Tash, I'm gonna go up and check on Mick. I love you."

"I love you, too."

I gave my youngest sister a hug, then went upstairs to see how Mick was doing. He'd seen his mother safely back in her apartment and then come here.

I knew he was still upset over seeing her in the hospital and I wanted to be there to comfort him.

"Hey, Millie sent up some of her famous beef stew and fresh bread. I told her how much you'd wanted some the other day," I said as I shut the door behind me.

I turned to see Mick sitting on the couch, an untouched beer bottle in front of him, staring unseeing at the TV.

I put the food down on the kitchen counter, then went back to the couch and crawled on his lap, snuggling him close and saying, "She's going to be okay."

"I know, she's just so stubborn," Mick said, squeezing me closer.

"Hmmm, sounds like the apple didn't fall far from the tree," I joked, trying to lighten his mood.

"No matter what I say, she won't agree to move in with me. I really think it would be better for her. Lord knows, I'd feel better."

"All you can do is keep asking."

"I had an idea . . . I could finish the basement for her. Put in a full-on apartment down there, so she could have all the luxuries she has at the facility, and have me right there if she needs anything. Maybe if I get it all fixed up and show it to her, she'll finally change her mind."

"That's a great idea. I didn't realize you had a basement."

"Yeah, there's not much down there but storage right now, but if I fixed it up, it'd be real nice. It's a walk out, so she wouldn't need to come up and down the stairs to go outside. We could put a sweet little deck out there, give her a nice spot to read."

"You should do it," I whispered, thinking I'd love to see the before and after. After all, I'd seen his kitchen and bathrooms, so knew he had the talent and ability to make something really special for Dottie.

"Do you? I wanted to get your input . . . to know if you're on board with her moving in," he asked, kissing the top of my head softly.

"Why wouldn't I? You certainly don't need my permission," I replied, looking up at him.

"Well, I think I do, because I'm hoping that one day you'll be living in that house with me, and I need to know that you wouldn't mind Ma living in an apartment downstairs," Mick replied, blowing my mind.

"Really?" I asked excitedly.

"Absolutely. That's where this is going for me, Dru. A house, marriage, kids, the whole shebang."

I switched position so that I was straddling him and kissed him with every ounce of love and happiness I had inside of me. His hands went under my shirt and caressed my bare back, simultaneously pulling me closer, so there wasn't an inch between us.

Mick undid my bra as I lifted the hem of his shirt, and we moved slightly apart so he could put his hands behind his head and grasp the back of his shirt. He pulled it off in one swift move, while I rid myself of my blouse and bra.

Crushing my naked breasts against his chest, I fisted my hands in his hair and kissed him again, rocking against his already hard cock and making us both moan.

Mick shifted beneath me, turning us so that I was laying back on the couch and he was laying over me, then began to work on the button and zipper of my skirt. I lifted my hips to help him ease it over my hips, then watched greedily as he undid his jeans and kicked them off.

My panties were next, then his boxer briefs, and finally he was laying back over me, his mouth on my breast and his hand moving over my hip.

I kissed him hungrily as I opened my legs wide, flinging one over the back of the couch and placing the other foot on the floor, so he was lined up right where I needed him. Mick kept his breathtaking green eyes on me as he slid slowly inside, my breath catching when he filled me fully.

I wrapped my legs around his waist, tucking my feet under the inside of his calves, and he began to slowly move.

Mick took my hands in his and intertwined our fingers, bringing them up over my head, his eyes never leaving mine as he thrust in and out, as if he had all the time in the world.

It was glorious torture, and I never wanted it to end.

He brushed his lips softly over mine, then said, "I love you, Druscilla."

Tears filled my eyes and I tried to blink them back, but one fell down my temple as I admitted, "I love you, too, Mick. So much."

We made love slowly, learning and loving every inch of each other's bodies. And when we came, it was like the stars aligned and confirmed we were meant to be together. Mick kissed the tears from my cheeks, and made me feel like the most precious being alive.

I knew that every second of my life had been leading me to this moment . . . to Mick.

Thirty-Four

Mick

"There's something important we need to discuss," Dru said from the bottom of the stairwell. "I know you're busy with the renovations, but we're running out of time, so I need to get you on board."

"With what?" I asked, pausing from putting the cabinets on what would hopefully be my mom's new kitchenette. "What's going on?"

"Well, Millie and I are turning thirty this month," she said, talking with her hands like she only did when she was excited.

"Yeah, I remember when your birthday is, babe," I replied with a smile.

"You know the date, but I don't think you realize how much I like to celebrate my birthday. This isn't just any birthday, it's a big one. Plus, last year Millie and I had separate birthday celebrations, but this year we are back together, just as it should be. So, we have to go big," Dru said, her eyes widening to alarming proportions. "And, Mick, I'm not only talking about a party . . . I'm talking about *the* party. And I don't just celebrate my birthday, but I celebrate my birthday *month*."

"Oh boy," I muttered, running my hand over my head.

Does that mean I'm supposed to get her presents every day of the month?

"Don't make that face," Dru said with a laugh. "I know what you're thinking. You don't have to do anything but be there for me on my birthday and come to the party."

"What about the rest of the month?" I asked, fearing the worst.

"It's no biggie, I just like to do little things for myself throughout the month, like get a massage, or take a day off and go to the lake. Stuff like that. I mean, if you want to throw some role playing, or kinky sex my way for my birthday month, I wouldn't say no."

"Really?" I asked, getting excited about this birthday month thing.

"Mmmm-hmmm," she said with a coy smile.

"Okay, well, if you need anything from me for the party, just let me know, but of course I'll be there. Where's it gonna be? Here? The bar?"

Dru rolled her eyes and I knew I was way off base.

"No, we're going to rent out the banquet room at The Hilton. Millie and I decided on an 80s theme, so all I need you to do is come up with a costume for yourself, we'll handle everything else."

"I can do that," I said, thinking of the old Def Leppard T-shirt I had stashed away in one of my drawers.

Seemed easy enough.

I watched her as she talked excitedly about her birthday, so beautiful and giving. In truth, Dru didn't ask for much, instead giving all of herself without expecting anything in return.

We'd been together over six months now, which may not seem like long to some, but when you were in your late thirties, like me, and you'd been around the block a few times, you recognized treasure when you found it.

And Dru was the treasure I'd been hunting for all my life.

Thinking the timing was right, I put down my tools, brushed the dust off my jeans, and walked over to where she was still happily talking about mix tapes, scrunchies, and neon clothes.

"Dru," I said softly.

She stopped talking and looked up on me, a residual smile on her face from her party planning.

"Yeah?"

"It's officially your birthday month now, right?"

Dru nodded.

I stopped in front of her and took her hands in mine.

"Move in with me," I said simply, looking into her eyes as they widened.

"What?" she gasped.

I clenched her hands in mine and grinned down at her.

"For your first birthday month gift, I think you should move in with me."

"That's not really how the birthday month works," she managed, biting her lip. "Are you serious?"

"I've never been more serious about anything in my life. We'll pack up your things and move you in this weekend. You can do whatever you want to the house . . . throw pillows, fuzzy blankets, plants . . . anything. Part of your birthday month celebration can include decorating our house. What do you say?"

Dru squealed and jumped up and down three times before pulling her hands from mine and wrapping them around my neck.

"*Yes, yes, yes!* I would love to move in with you."

We kissed, both of us smiling so hard that our lips barely touched.

"Ma's gonna be ecstatic," I told her. "She's already making wedding plans."

"I know," Dru replied with a chuckle. "Last time I was at her place, she randomly had bride magazines on her coffee table."

"Hmmm, subtle," I joked.

"If there's one thing your mother is not, it's subtle."

"That is true."

"Maybe my moving in will be in the plus column for her accepting this apartment," Dru said, looking around at the space that I was almost done working on.

"I doubt it. She'll probably argue that we need alone time, not her living under the same roof," I said, knowing the way my ma's brain worked.

"Don't worry," Dru said. "We'll convince her. Between the two of us, we're bound to wear her down."

Dru

"Gosh, I'm nervous . . . Why am I so nervous?"

I was pacing across Jericho and Tasha's living room, practically wearing a hole in their carpet.

"It's going to be fine, they'll love you," Millie assured me.

She was busying herself with food and refreshments, and I knew she'd already checked those canapes three times, so she wasn't fooling anyone. She was just as nervous about meeting our brothers as I was.

We were all there, with me, Millie, and Tasha waiting in the living room, while Mick, Jackson, and Jericho were hanging out on the back porch.

We'd decided to give the brothers a chance to meet us first, then bring in the guys once they were comfortable, so as not to overwhelm them on our first meeting.

"You're both making me nervous, come sit down," Tasha said, one hand on her protruding belly, and the other on the seat next to her.

I was about to join her when the doorbell rang.

"They're here!" I cried, freezing in place.

"Well, go let them in," Tasha said, shifting uncomfortably. "This is what you've been waiting for."

"Right," I replied, spinning on my heel and hurrying to the door.

I opened it to see three tall, good-looking young men who had our father's eyes and varying shades of brown hair.

"Hi, I'm Dru, welcome and please come in."

I cringed at how mechanical I sounded. I planned parties for a living for crying out loud, I should have no problem talking to people.

Except, these weren't just people, they were the brothers I never knew I had.

I stood back while they walked inside. Brody was the last one in, and he totally put me at ease when he stopped and hugged me quickly.

"Hi, Dru, thanks for inviting us to come over," he said with his sweet, lopsided grin.

"Thanks for coming, Brody. I'm a little nervous," I admitted softly.

"Me too . . . we all are. We must have tried on fifty different shirts between us," Brody whispered back.

I smiled at him and closed the door as I followed them into the living room where Millie and Tasha were introducing themselves.

"I'm Ridge, and this is Wes and Brody," the tallest, and I assumed oldest, brother was saying.

"We're so happy you could come, are you hungry? Care for a drink?" Millie asked, taking Ridge toward the small buffet she'd set up.

"How far along are you, Natasha?" Wes, the middle brother, asked.

"Please, call me Tasha. I'm just over six months," she replied, rubbing her belly lovingly.

"Cool," Brody said. "I've always wanted to be an uncle."

Tasha's face brightened and I knew she hadn't thought of that yet.

"Well, you're in luck, cause you're about to be."

"I can't tell you how shocked we were when Brody told us that he'd found out we had older sisters. I can't believe our father kept that from us, although I really shouldn't be surprised by anything he does any more," Ridge said, his tone conveying his anger when he mentioned our dad.

"I'm sorry they decided to keep it from us, I would have loved the chance to know you growing up, but, as I'm sure you know, after our dad left us, he never looked back." Millie's eyes filled as she spoke. "Sorry."

"You don't have to apologize," Ridge said. "Our dad is a dick, always had been, always will be. I'm glad my mom's finally getting shot of him, even though she's not much better. From what I hear, you guys at least lucked out in the mom department."

"Yeah, we really did," Tasha said with a wistful smile. "I'm sorry you didn't at least have that."

"At least we'll have each other, right?" Brody said, all wide-eyed and optimistic. "I'm thinking this house probably looks pretty badass for Christmas."

"Brody," Wes chided, as if Brody was going too far by inviting himself to come back.

"He's fine, Wes," I assured him. "Honestly, we're happy to have you back anytime you want to come. Holidays, breaks, the weekend, whenever you want to visit. You're family, and you're always welcome."

"Thanks," Ridge said, popping a jalapeno popper into his mouth.

"Wes and I are at U of M, and Brody will be joining us in the fall, so we don't get a lot of time off, but thanks for the invite."

"It's open-ended," Millie replied, shooting me a look that said, Ridge would be the tough nut to crack.

"If you guys don't mind, our husbands and my boyfriend are here and would love to meet you as well. Then we can all sit down and eat," I said, trying to read their expressions to see how things were going.

"Yeah, I'd like to meet 'em. Mick's your boyfriend, right, Dru? The PI our mom hired?" Wes asked, surprising me a little.

"Uh, yeah, I didn't know she'd told you about that."

"My mom tells me everything."

"Yeah, he's the favorite," Brody said with a grin.

"Shut up, Brody," was Wes's reply.

I could hear Brody's big laugh as I went out to grab the men.

"Hey, you can come in now," I said, then looked around and saw they were doing just fine, chilling with whiskey and cigars out on the patio.

"Okay, we'll be right in," Mick replied, before taking a puff off of his cigar.

Mick

*E*verywhere I looked there were leg warmers, lace gloves, and big, ratted-out hair dos.

Toto played over the speaker and everyone looked to be having the time of their lives.

The sisters had really outdone themselves for the twins' birthday, turning this banquet room into a time machine and taking us all back to the eighties.

I had on my regular jeans and Def Leppard T-shirt, and that was as far as my costume went, but some of the guests had gone all out. From my vantage point by the open bar, I could see a Michael Jackson, Prince, Bon Jovi, and what someone had described as Rainbow Bright.

Dru was dressed up as *Like a Virgin, Madonna*, and had been working the room ever since we'd arrived.

She was laughing at something that Brody said, her face lit up with happiness. It was a good look on her, and one that I hoped I'd see often throughout our lives.

Jackson and Millie, who were dressed as Mork and Mindy, were dancing their way across the floor. I chuckled as I watched Jackson try to Moonwalk, then took the old fashioned the bartender had just finished over to where Ma was sitting.

She was dressed just like she normally was, and when I commented on her not wearing a costume, she'd replied, "I'm one of the Golden Girls."

"Here you go," I said, placing the cocktail in front of Ma and a bottle of water in front of Tasha, who was also dressed in her regular clothes.

"I'm a pregnant TV mom, take your pick," she'd said wryly, clearly not feeling up to the festivities.

"Gah, this baby won't stop playing soccer with my bladder," Tasha complained, pushing herself up to standing, then heading to the bathroom. Again.

"That sucks," I said as I sat next to Ma.

"What?" she asked, taking a sip of her drink and nodding in approval.

"Being pregnant. Tash is miserable."

Ma waved her hand.

"It'll pass. Pregnancy has its ups and downs, but the payoff is huge. You'll see," she said, giving me the side eye.

"One step at a time, Ma. Dru just moved in."

"I mean, better to live as husband and wife than to live in sin, but who am I to judge?" Ma replied, and I knew she didn't really care about Dru and I living together without being married, she just really wanted us to get married and start a family.

I understood. Having me later in life meant she wasn't getting any younger, and she wanted to be around for as much of her grandchildren's life as she could.

Which was only one of the reasons why I was planning

something big for Dru's birthday present.

"Need anything to eat?" I asked as I stood up, intent on the buffet.

"Some of those meatballs and little egg roll things."

"You got it."

On my way to the food, I saw Miami Vice, aka, Jericho and Hector, surveying the food and Millie mixing something in a big punch bowl. I took a detour to her.

"You and Jackson sure know how to cut a rug," I said with a grin.

Millie laughed prettily, and I moved to kiss her on the cheek.

"Happy birthday," I said, pulling a small box out of my pocket that contained a necklace with a rose gold whisk-shaped pendant.

"Oh, Mick, you shouldn't have," Millie said, taking the box and opening the lid. "Oh, wow, it's beautiful. Thank you so much."

"You're welcome," I said, then, embarrassed by the emotion I was feeling I asked, "What are you making?"

"Eggnog," she said, taking the necklace out of the box and placing it around her neck, then turning slightly so I could clasp the back.

"Eggnog, it's not Christmas."

Millie patted the necklace with a small smile on her lips, then said, "I know it's not Christmas, obviously, but it is my birthday, and I love eggnog, so, why not?"

"I've never been much of a fan," I admitted.

"That's because you've never tried mine. Here . . ."

"Hey, *big stud*," Dru said, coming up next to me and wrapping her arms around my waist.

"Hey, birthday girl."

I took the cup Millie offered and took a sip.

"Huh, it doesn't taste all thick and sweet like that stuff you get at the grocery store," I commented, taking another sip.

It was creamy, slightly sweet, with a kick. I liked it.

"That's the vanilla," Dru said, grinning at her sister as she filled her own cup.

"Vanilla? I thought whiskey was the secret ingredient to egg-nog," I joked.

"Oh, there's whiskey in there too, but I've found that a splash of vanilla elevates the eggnog from a perfectly good drink to an excellent one."

"Nice," I said, surprising myself by finishing the cup. "I'll have to have Ma try this, she'll love it."

"I'll take her some," Millie offered.

"I'm grabbing her some meatballs and spring rolls anyways, so . . ."

"On it," Millie countered, walking away to fix my ma a plate.

"I didn't know she was so bossy," I told Dru, who was grinning up at me.

"I think being Kayla's mom has helped with that."

"Dance with me," I murmured.

When she beamed at me and nodded, I took her hand and led her to the center of the floor.

We danced to some horrible eighties song that had me yearning for a little Pink Floyd, but I blocked it out and focused on the woman in my arms. Scanning the room, I saw that everyone was there, including all of Dru's brothers, so I stopped dancing and took both of her hands in mine.

"Why'd you stop?" she asked, meeting my eyes.

"Dru, Druscilla," I began, fighting to keep the emotion out of my voice. "You came crashing into my life like a jackhammer, and while I stuck to my code of not dating clients, you waited patiently until you could bust down my walls and sneak inside. You're the balance that I needed in my life. The light to my dark. The Madonna to my Bob Dylan. You're the splash of vanilla I didn't know I needed to make my content life exceptional."

I paused and got down on one knee, releasing her right hand to pull the other jewelry box out of my pocket.

I looked up to see Dru staring down at me, tears streaming down her face with an expression of wonder.

"Dru, will you make me the luckiest man alive and marry me?"

She mouthed the word *yes,* but no sound came out.

That's good enough for me.

I slid the ring on her finger and stood, taking her in my arms as she found her voice and shouted, "Yes!"

The room erupted in cheers as I hugged her and spun in a circle.

I searched out Ma, found her crying and laughing with Millie and Tasha, and closed my eyes as I hugged my bride to be.

"I love you," I whispered.

"I love you, too," Dru replied, cupping my face with her hands. "I'm gonna be the best wife ever."

"All I need you to be, is you."

Epilogue

Dru

"I am so hungry, I could eat three cheeseburgers, but my belly feels so full of baby that I can't imagine trying to fit anything else in there . . . It's the weirdest feeling"

Tasha was in her last few weeks of pregnancy and had reached the *get it out* stage.

We were at a barbecue at Tasha and Jericho's house. Millie and I had come early to cook and help get everything ready, so Tasha didn't have to. She wanted to stay close to home, so we brought the party to her.

She was sitting in her rocking chair on the porch, holding court while we all buzzed around her.

Our brothers couldn't make it down, since they all had school, but we kept in contact with messages and social media. The whole gang was here though, as we celebrated Tasha and Jericho's last few days of freedom, before their lives were taken over by the new baby.

"Burgers are done!" Jericho called out from behind the grill he was manning. "Brats and dogs are up next."

"Is there anything I can do for you?" I asked, feeling bad for her.

Tasha sighed.

"Can you get him out?"

I laughed and shook my head.

"I'm afraid that's one thing I can't do," I replied, then patted her shoulder before going to where Mick was sitting with his ma, Millie, Jackson, Rob, Jan, Ty, Rebecca, Hector, and Tanisha.

"Hey, babe, want me to make you a burger?" I asked, coming up behind him and placing my hands on his shoulders.

"That's okay, I'll get it. I was just trying to convince Ma she should move in with us. The apartment is sitting there empty, waiting for her to fill it with magazines, hot Funyons, and Judge Judy."

This was a discussion I'd heard a million times over the last few months.

"I bet I can get her to say yes," I told him with a sly grin.

"Be my guest," Mick replied skeptically.

I moved over to his ma's seat and crouched down, then leaned in and whispered in her ear. Then, I stood up, stepped back, and waited.

"How soon can you pack up my stuff?" she asked Mick, totally straight-faced.

He gaped at her.

"What?"

"You'd better not damage anything, and I want everything set up *exactly* like I have it in my place now."

"Are you serious? You'll move in?"

"Just try and stop me."

Mick swung his wide eyes gaze to me, and I smiled down into the beautiful face of the man who'd given me everything I'd ever wanted.

"What did you say to her?" he asked.

"Oh, only that she'd get more time with the baby if she lived under the same roof."

"What?" He stood up so quickly his chair toppled over, then he reached for me, before snatching his hands back and looking down at my abdomen. "You're *pregnant?*"

"Yes, *we* are," I replied, trying not to cry, even though everything seemed to hit me right in the feels. "And, I'm not fragile, you can touch me."

"Are you sure?" he asked, looking down at his large hands.

"Positive," I said, stepping in to hug him tightly.

"Thank you."

"For what?"

"For loving me. For giving me a family. For allowing me to have my *whole* family under one roof," he murmured as he held me gently.

"I'll give you everything, everything that's in my power to give," I promised him.

"And I, you."

Dru

"I've got the tequila," Tasha called as she walked into the now-closed storefront of Three Sisters.

"Perfect," Millie said, leaning back in her chair with a sigh. "I figured that's what you'd pick over champagne, so I went with chips and fresh salsa, rather than macaroons."

"You know me so well," Tasha replied with a wink, setting the bottle and three shot glasses on the table.

Our husbands were taking care of the kids so that we could celebrate the five-year anniversary of Three Sisters Catering together, much as we'd toasted the opening five years ago . . . just the three of us.

"Ah, it feels so good to be off my feet," Millie said, closing her eyes briefly.

She'd been in the kitchen all day prepping for a family reunion the next day.

She and Jackson had waited a few years before having children, content with letting Kayla and Millie get used to their new roles. Last year they'd had Dexter, and the three of them doted on the sweet baby boy.

"I hear that," I said, having worked a promotion event earlier in the afternoon.

Tasha poured the three shots of tequila and divvied them up between us.

Her son, Isaac, was a little hellion, and she and Jericho had been on the fence as to whether or not they wanted more kids. I was pretty sure they'd end up with at least one more, if not two. After all, at least one of us should have a little girl, so Kayla wasn't the lone girl anymore.

My and Mick's son, Michael III, was his father's heart and my soul. The sweetest, yet toughest kid I'd ever seen. We'd decided to start trying again in the next few months, so little Mickie would have a brother or sister to grow up with. For now, he was content to hang out with his cousins.

We'd gotten to know our brothers well over the years, and I loved to see them interacting with the children. They were really good with them. Of course, they all have their own lives, and their own stories, but that's for them to tell.

"To Three Sisters," Millie said, raising her glass. "It's more than I ever dreamed it could be, and I'm so grateful that I've had the two of you along with me on this crazy ride. I love you guys."

"Yes, and to finding the perfect staff to help us make our dreams a reality, and our ever-so-patient husbands for putting up with our crazy schedules," Tasha added.

"Finally," I said. "To Mom, whose absence is always felt. We miss you, Momma, and hope we've made you proud."

"*Salude*," we chimed, raising our glasses a little higher before throwing the shot back.

The chimes in the window made a beautiful melody, even though the windows were closed, and I knew it was our mother joining in the celebration.

She always did love tequila.

The End.

Did you enjoy the Three Sisters Catering trilogy? Check out the first chapter of *Too Tempting*, book 1 in The Lewis Cousins series.

TOO TEMPTING

ONE

Gabe

I took a deep breath as I walked out of my cabin and onto the wooden deck overlooking the lake and forty wooded acres of my camp.

I'd built *Camp Gabriel Lewis* over three years ago, after I'd retired from the NFL and decided to make my dream of working with teens a reality. My camp was not just a football camp, and not just your traditional sleepaway camp; it was a combination of both. It was the culmination of a vision I had when I was a young kid, and the only things I gave a *damn* about in life were football and my annual camping trip with my cousins.

"Son of a bitch, it's good to be back here!" I grinned over my ceramic coffee mug at my cousin, Reardon, who'd just pulled in.

Crazy tall, blond, and charismatic, he was the person I'd been closest to growing up. My best friend. Now he was a lawyer in the small town he grew up in.

"Happy to get away from the hustle and bustle of Cherry Springs?" I asked with a chuckle.

"No, man, things there are quiet as usual," Reardon responded as he pulled his duffle bag from the trunk of his Mercedes. "I'm just looking forward to kicking your ass at family sports day this year."

"You wish, cupcake," I responded wryly, feeling ridiculously happy to see him again.

"Hey, I've been working out," he countered with a grin.

When he reached the top we came together in a quick hug, each giving the other a sharp clap on the back before pulling apart.

"C'mon, I'll walk you down to your cabin so you can get settled in. Jasmine and Dillon are en route. They'll probably get in tonight. Serena had to work today, but said she should be in first thing in the morning."

"Sounds good."

I followed him back down the steps and onto the trail, which led to the row of cabins. The counselors stay in the cabins when camp is in session, but my family always lived in them when we came down for our annual trip the week before opening.

"This is you, as usual," I said, jogging up the steps to open the door, since his hands were full. "So, what have you been doing since Easter?" I asked as he tossed the bag effortlessly onto the bed.

"Had a couple cases, nothing really exciting," he replied, opening the drawers to the dresser so he could unpack.

"Things still good with Brenda . . . or was it Bonnie?" I asked, honestly unable to remember the name of the girl he'd brought for Easter dinner.

"It's Becca, *and no*, we broke up."

When I looked at him pointedly, asking him what happened without saying the words, he shrugged.

"She liked the idea of being with a lawyer, but not living in a small town. She kept trying to convince me to move to the city . . . kept leaving brochures around and shit. I finally told her that leaving was not an option for me, and she bailed."

"That sucks, Rear, I'm sorry things didn't work out," I said sincerely. Neither of us had ever been married. In our twenties, we'd enjoyed playing the field, but we'd recently agreed that we were ready to stop all the bullshit and settle down.

Unfortunately, the kind of women we seemed to attract weren't the kind that we wanted to marry. Now we were older, and set in our ways, we were finding that women our age were set in theirs too, so it was difficult to find someone who wanted the same things we did.

"It's for the best," he replied, rolling his bag up and shoving it in the closet. "It's better to find out now, than when I proposed, right?"

"Was it that serious?"

"I don't know . . . It could have been."

I looked my cousin over, determined he didn't look heartbroken or anything, and figured he was better off. He'd find the right woman soon enough, but for now, it was time to enjoy a week with our favorite people.

"I was just about to take a look around, see if anything needs to be fixed," I said, tilting my head toward the door. "You wanna head out?"

"Yeah, sounds good. Let me just hit the head real quick and we can take off on foot."

I went back out onto the porch to let him take a piss in peace. These cabins had their own bathrooms, and were usually shared by two counselors of the same sex. Once you got to the part of camp where the campers stayed, there were communal bathrooms and showers. Each of those cabins had five bunk beds, and a twin bed for the junior counselors.

"All right, let's do this," Reardon said as he rushed outside, the screen door slapping as it closed.

We took off at a brisk pace as we walked. I was probably three inches shorter than Reardon, but even though I was retired, I still kept myself in pretty good shape. My cousin was no slouch by any means, but he did spend a lot of time behind a desk. Even though he knew I was faster than him, and almost always came out on top in any competition, Reardon was still the most competitive person I knew. That was why, after less than a half mile of him trying to walk faster than me, he took off at a sprint, his laughter floating behind him.

"Really?" I shouted. "You're starting this shit already?"

Then I was off, running at full speed and gaining on him within moments. Right before we reached the break in the trees to the center of main camp, I gave it an extra push and passed him with a whoop.

I stopped at the flagpole, hands on my knees as I looked up at him, laughing at his red-faced scowl.

"When you gonna give it up?" I asked good-naturedly. A big part of our relationship included giving each other a hard time.

"Never," he vowed, like he always did, then held his side. "I think I caught a cramp."

"Serves you right, cupcake."

Reardon shook his head as he looked around.

"The place looks great."

"I had a team come in about a month ago. Did general landscaping and maintenance. Made sure everything was on point for opening day. I've used them before, so I knew they'd do the job I hired 'em to do, but a lot can go wrong in a month. I want to make sure that at some point this week we put eyes on every facility. Make sure nothing broke, fell, or got eaten by a wild animal since they left."

"Sounds easy enough," he replied, then asked, "I know it's kind of early, but I'm starving. What are your plans for dinner tonight?"

"I was thinking we could either do brats or steaks. I picked up a tri tip too, but figured we could save that for the last night."

"That sounds good, and for tonight, steaks sound perfect."

"We can head back and get the grill fired up. I can always hop on the four wheeler and take a quick turn around the camp before dinner."

"Perfect."

We were headed back toward our cabins when the sound of leaves crunching had me bracing and looking to my left.

The last thing I expected to see was a leggy brunette in cut-offs and a tank top come walking out of the woods. Being an hour away from the closest town meant we didn't often get unexpected visitors, but I was more curious than worried when she spotted us and relief flooded her face.

"Hey," she said, her low, throaty voice open and friendly. "I'm so happy to see you guys. I parked back in the welcome lot, which is empty by the way, and have been growing more and more worried. This *is* Camp Gabriel Lewis, right? I'm supposed to be filling in for my sister as chaperone for the week while my nephew's here at camp."

I took in her big brown eyes and long dark hair, which was currently going wild and trying to escape its ponytail, then shot Reardon a look before turning back to her and replying, "I hate to say it, darlin', but camp doesn't start until next week."

About the Author

Award-Winning Author Bethany Lopez began self-publishing in June 2011. She's a lover of all things romance: books, movies, music, and life, and she incorporates that into the books she writes. When she isn't reading or writing, she loves spending time with her husband and children, traveling whenever possible. Some of her favorite things are: Kristen Ashley Books, coffee in the morning, and In N Out burgers.

CONNECT WITH ME:

www.bethanylopezauthor.com

Facebook, Goodreads, Pinterest, Google +,Tumblr, Instagram

Acknowledgements

Thanks to Allie at Makeready Designs for the beautiful cover for this book, and for the whole series. The brand is amazing.

Thanks to Lori, Christine, Ann, Raine, and Becky for your wonderful feedback.

Thanks to Kristina at Red Road Editing and Kay and KMS Editing, for editing and proofing A Splash of Vanilla and getting it ready for the readers.

Thanks to Christine of Type A Formatting for making the inside and pretty as the outside.

Thanks to my ARC Readers and Bombshells for reading my books and loving my characters.

Finally, thanks to my family, for your constant support. I couldn't do anything without you by my side.